OMNIVM LVX CIVIVM

BOSTON
PUBLIC
LIBRARY

ALICE
with Golden Hair

ALICE
with Golden Hair

Eleanor Hull

Atheneum   1981   *New York*

Library of Congress Cataloging in Publication Data

Hull, Eleanor
    Alice with golden hair.

    Summary: An eighteen-year-old mentally retarded girl finds
friendship, a feeling of self-worth, but also many problems
of understanding and adjustment when she takes a job in a
nursing home.
    [1.   Mentally handicapped—Fiction.   2.   Aged—
Fiction.   3.   Nursing homes—Fiction]   I.   Title.
PZ7.H8775Al   [Fic]   81–2214
ISBN 0–689–30845–0   AACR2

Published simultaneously in Canada by
McClelland & Stewart, Ltd.
Composed by American–Stratford Graphic Services, Inc.
Brattleboro, Vermont
Manufactured by R. R. Donnelley & Sons, Inc.
Crawfordsville, Indiana

Designed by Maria Epes

First Edition

To Ann and Harry, in appreciation

ALICE
with Golden Hair

1

"REMEMBER, Alice you have to be ready for your interview at ten o'clock tomorrow morning," said the cottage mother, poking her head through the bathroom door as Alice was brushing her teeth.

It was a shock. Alice felt as if her whole insides had gone away.

Ten o'clock. That was not very early—she thought—but she was sure it must be before noon. Noon was when Alice always got up on Saturday, and tomorrow was Saturday. She loved Saturday; it was so nice to wake up at the usual time and then remember, and stretch and wriggle around in bed and go to sleep again. Sleeping was really nicer than being awake.

But the worst part was what was going to happen at ten o'clock. "Interview," the cottage mother had called it. She hadn't said what an interview was, or why Alice was going to have one. But it had to be connected with the fact, rubbed into the older girls all the time now, that they were about to "graduate."

Alice went to bed, but she couldn't fall asleep. The interview waited on the other side of the night, like a big dog hiding behind a wall.

Alice heard Miss—what was her name?—sneak in to set Alice's alarm clock. Alice couldn't remember her name, because she wanted them to call her "Mike," as if they had no right to know her real name. As if she were another girl like them. But she wasn't a girl, she had gray hair. And of course, she wasn't retarded.

Mike tiptoed out again, and then left for the evening. She slipped through the door and crept down the steps, got into her car quietly and let it coast silently down the slanting drive before she switched on the engine. But when she turned into the road the lights made a pattern on the ceiling.

Mike thought she was so smart; she didn't realize that everyone knew when she left. Some of the girls would sneak out when she was gone. If Alice had had a sport for a roommate, she might have done it, but Morgana was too scared. Well, Alice was scared, too. And of course, anyway, Alice wouldn't want to get too chummy with a Colored.

Alice went on worrying about the interview. She knew it must mean she would have to go to some strange place and sit in a chair by herself and have people ask her questions. This had happened so many times since Mama got sick and Daddy first put her away. (But she wouldn't think about that.)

But she couldn't stop thinking about tomorrow. She could already feel those people staring at her. Not just at her but into her. Anywhere, they could look; between her legs, if they wanted, down her neck. Through her eyes right into the middle of her head.

4

She woke up to the hateful burr of the alarm.

"Congrats, Alice!" cried Mike, sticking her red smiling face in at the door. "You're going out into the world today! Really growing up! I'm proud of you. Now, up and at 'em! Pancakes for breakfast."

Alice thought about turning over and pretending to go back to sleep. But Mike would just come and drag her out and be mad at her, and she'd have to go anyway. It was hopeless. Alice got up and began to dress.

"Oh. Not your blue jeans, Kid," said Mike, peeping around the door to check up on her. "You want to make a good impression. Just think of maybe having a job of your very own!"

Alice felt cold all over. A job of her very own! How could they possibly think she could do it? "Are you going with me?"

"Well, you know I'm not. I can't leave the others. Mrs. Hones will come and pick you up."

Mrs. Hones had probably fixed up the whole thing.

Mrs. Hones was late.

"Where is she?" said Mike, after pacing around waiting for a long time, while Alice huddled on the edge of her bed. "Doesn't she realize that punctuality is something employers always make a point of?" Mike was always punctual, which meant she was always waiting for somebody.

Mike often got mad at Mrs. Hones and muttered after she left. That was because when Mrs. Hones came she told Mike what to do. Or not to do.

"Here she comes," said Alice. All too soon, Alice thought.

"Put on your coat, Alice, it's snappy out," said Mrs.

5

Hones, dashing in. "Hurry. I've got a million things to do today."

Alice followed her to the door, struggling into her coat as she went. Mrs. Hones didn't help her. Mrs. Hones didn't like her. When she first met Mrs. Hones, quite a while ago, Alice had been surprised that she was going to have someone like that to tell her what to do. "You're Colored," she had said.

"Black," snapped Mrs. Hones, and she had had it in for Alice ever since. She never did something nice like other social workers, who sometimes took the kids to a movie or something.

Mrs. Hones was probably hoping this interview would help her get rid of Alice for once and all. It would be nice for Mrs. Hones, and for Mike, to get Alice off their hands. But then, where would Alice be, and how would she manage?

She could just say she wouldn't go, but then they might try to send her home. She would never go home. Never. Never.

Alice pushed that thought out of her head and began to look around. She rather liked the ride down the parkway. She didn't get many rides. Just the annual picnic, and when some church took all the kids to a party.

Today was still winter, snappy, as Mrs. Hones had said. But it was almost spring. Alice knew that from the bushes. There were no leaves on them yet, but they kind of glowed. The bark must have changed color.

"There's a robin!" she said.

Mrs. Hones kept her eyes on the road. "Oh, there's a robin, is there?"

She turned off the parkway. "Let's not think about robins. Look, I want you to be very careful in this interview. It's a good opportunity, and I don't want you to botch it. Some of these nursing homes for the elderly are a mess, I know. I have clients in a lot of them. But this is newly remodeled, with all the most modern equipment and nice rooms for everybody. I don't have any clients there now, but I have had, and it's the best. They even have a dormitory for their help. You'll be lucky if they take you."

"They'll be lucky if they get me!" Alice was just imitating Sheila, because she knew it would get Mrs. Hones's goat. But her voice sounded hollow. Get her for what? Take her for what? Mrs. Hones said the place was for old people—what had it to do with her?

Mrs. Hones controlled herself. Alice could feel her doing it.

They turned onto the bluff that overlooked the river. The houses were large and grand. One of the largest stood on a sloping lawn with lots of trees around it; but it looked strange, because two new wings were patched onto the pillared front.

Mrs. Hones turned the car into a drive with a roof over it. Alice had never seen so fancy an entrance. You would be able to go from the car to the house without a drop of rain falling on you.

Neat bushes and hedges grew around the porch, and green spears of daffodils were pricking through the black earth. The steps were of brick and the door was white with a window above it like a fan opened wide. Mrs. Hones turned the doorknob, and a chime rang in the hall.

The hall had a familiar look, shabby, homey, but not

7

really belonging to anybody. Nobody sat in the old chairs or the sofa with the flowered slipcover, and the large foliage plant with saw-toothed leaves was not real. There was a gate across the bottom of the great curved stairway.

What was really going on was business: a woman typing, through the door at the left. Mrs. Hones led Alice in through the door.

"Hi! Well, we finally got here. Mrs. Leaming, this is Alice."

"McMartin," said Alice. She was old enough so people ought to use her last name.

"Well, Miss McMartin!" said Mrs. Leaming as if it were a joke. "Mr. Bell will be ready to see you presently. Won't you sit down?"

"Yes indeedy," said Mrs. Hones, dropping promptly into one of the chintzy armchairs. "I take advantage of every opportunity! Run, run, run, all day long. I wish my clients were all in one place and practically dead, like yours."

"Well, dear, that's not such an advantage, really," Mrs. Leaming answered reprovingly. "As you very well know. I'd be only too glad if they were a little livelier. And they do require a great deal of attention—like children, only harder to handle."

"Harder to handle than children!" Mrs. Hones protested. "God Almighty! My daughter has taken a dislike to her first-grade teacher. I can hardly get her to school. I have to escort her to the school door and hand her over to some-body. And the look she gives me! As if I'm throwing her to the lions. Sometimes I wonder if I'm not."

"Well, you hate to see them unhappy, but their only hope

8

in life is to learn to adjust. I know how you feel, though. I had the same trouble with my youngest son."

They talked on about their children, and Alice lost track. She usually listened to everything people said, trying to puzzle out what was happening, but today she was too nervous.

Her heart was still thumping, but not quite so hard. It no longer seemed to her that she was, as Mrs. Hones had said of her daughter, being led into a lion's den. Nothing so exciting as that. Everything was ordinary—the desk, the typewriter, the slouching boy who went down the hall pushing a dust mop over the asphalt tile. The knots in her stomach were loosening. Just the same stuff over again. Except that here she was a stranger.

Out in the lobby she saw a bulletin board just like the one at the Home, with white letters that slid into grooves to spell whatever was wanted. Alice could read most of it: MONDAY . . . BINGO. (At the home they weren't allowed Bingo. It was a game of chance.) TUESDAY . . . RELIGIOUS SERVICES. (That meant church.) FRIDAY . . . BIRTHDAY PARTY. That was the same—one party each month for all the people who'd had a birthday. But these parties would be for old people!

As if to prove this, an old woman came down the hall and limped over to the bulletin board. She stood leaning on her cane as she looked at it. Alice could see her lips moving as she read. The old woman's profile was as white and bony as a skeleton. It reminded Alice of fish bones that have been scattered on the ground by a cat in the garbage pail. While Alice watched, the old woman lifted her handkerchief with a trembling hand and wiped the drool from her mouth.

9

At the same moment, Mrs. Leaming slightly raised her voice, and Alice realized she was being addressed.

"Well, dear, I hope you like old people. Do you think you might want to help us take care of them?"

Alice finally realized for sure what they meant her to do. To look after horrible old things like this, who drooled and shook and probably smelled! She wouldn't do it.

She didn't have to! She could refuse! And if they paid no attention to her "no"—a word that meant so much less from her lips than from theirs—she could fight. She could scream. She could go off into a trance. She hadn't done any of these things for quite a while, but she still remembered how.

They would say, "Aren't you ashamed! A grownup girl acting like a baby." And then, "You can't get away with this, you know!" And then some kind of punishment. But what did she care? Whatever they did, they couldn't make her arms and legs do the things she didn't want them to.

The old lady was turning around. She limped right through the door into the office. Just as if she were a real person.

She stood there a minute, looking them all over, all three of them. Mrs. Hones and Mrs. Leaming stopped talking and waited for her to go away. But she didn't, only kept on looking and kind of smiled.

"Oh, hello, Mrs. Daniels. How are you today?" said Mrs. Leaming after quite a long silence.

The old lady didn't bother to answer. She was staring at Alice.

"Mrs. Daniels, this is Alice. We're hoping she's going to come and be a helper here."

10

"So, a helper!" said the old lady, and she laughed. Her laugh startled Alice. It was a bit hoarse, but not feeble. "Alice! Good enough! . . . *And Alice with golden hair.*"

Then she turned around and limped away.

Mrs. Leaming said, "What a case she is! Always something to say."

"Oh? I thought you were just wishing they had more life," said Mrs. Hones.

"There's life and life," said Mrs. Leaming.

"I wonder," said Mrs. Hones.

"Well, anyway, she was right this time," said Mrs. Leaming, smiling playfully at Alice. "Alice does have very pretty hair, doesn't she?"

"It would be even nicer if she'd brush and take care of it," said Mrs. Hones.

Alice had been sitting with her mouth open, astonished at all this comment. Mrs. Hones brought her back to earth. She was used to being jawed at about neatness.

The buzzer rang. Mrs. Leaming pressed a button. "Yes, Mr. Bell . . . I'll bring them right in."

So this was it. Alice's heart began to thump again as she followed the women into an office that was roomy and quiet, with high ceilings and recessed windows. Beyond a green carpet was a great big desk, with a shiny empty surface like a lake.

The man on the other side of the desk was looking at her in a narrow-eyed way. He was a little older than young, but his face was plump, like a boy's. His hair was gray in front of his ears, but that only made his complexion more rosy and soft.

"So this is Alice," he said.

"Alice McMartin," said Alice. It came out in a whisper. "You're rather young."

Alice had nothing to say about that. Mrs. Hones answered for her. "She'll be eighteen in two weeks. Legal working age."

"Well, let's see," said Mr. Bell. He was looking into a folder that Alice recognized as her own file. He pursed up his lips as if what he saw displeased him.

Mrs. Hones said, "Occasionally Alice has acted out, shown some aggressive behavior. But not for a long time now. And never more than anyone might do in like circumstances."

Acting out. That meant jumping around, hitting out and yelling, or falling down in a fit, which Alice knew how to do very well. But she'd gotten tired of it. It never got her anything but scolding and a headache.

"Well, we must remember that circumstances here are not always so great, either," said Mr. Bell.

"Alice has never been violent toward others. Just explosive tantrums sometimes. And as I say, she seems to have outgrown all that. She's one of our quietest girls."

"Good. Good. But by quiet, do you mean—well, can she handle things? You feel sure she's capable of doing what's required here?"

"Oh, yes. I must say they give them pretty good training at that home. They do all the domestic work there, except the cooking, of course. Laundry. Cleaning. The place is always neat as a pin. And I'm sure you give in-service training on the nursing end?"

"Of course. We have a very good training program. But

the aides do have to work pretty much on their own, when it comes to the job. I wonder, now, Alice, how you would manage," Mr. Bell said, leaning forward on the desk and looking at Alice severely. "Say, if a patient got very sick and you were all alone with her?"

Alice managed to keep her mouth from falling open, since they were all looking at her. (Some teacher had snapped at her years ago, "Shut your mouth! Do you want to look like the fool you are?") But light waves seemed to zigzag past Mr. Bell's face. What would she do? What *could* she do? Oh, this was awful.

"That's hardly a fair question, Mr. Bell," said Mrs. Hones. "Wait till she's had a touch of experience."

"Remember, Cheryl O'Brien left this morning," added Mrs. Leaming warningly. "We're very short-handed."

"She might not be able to take over tomorrow or the next day. But she's capable of learning," said Mrs. Hones. "Alice is quite high-grade, you know. IQ of 75, which is almost what we call normal."

". . . And Mrs. Vasty has pneumonia," said Mrs. Leaming.

"Hm," said Mr. Bell. "Well, I must say, Alice is very personable. A nice, quiet-looking girl. I guess she might do. Let's give her a try, anyway. And she wants to live in? She understands the terms?"

"Live in this place?" Alice said, the words shocked out of her.

"Oh, yes, upstairs in a dormitory with other young workers, it's very nice," said Mrs. Hones. She added hastily, "I guess we haven't really talked over this part. What would you say, Alice, to having all your living expenses paid, and besides that, fifty dollars a week for your very own?"

Fifty dollars a week! She'd never had more than five in her whole life. Shop windows and movie theaters floated before her mind's eye.

"And who would help her look after her money?" asked Mr. Bell. "Her family?"

"Under the circumstances, it seems wiser for me to," said Mrs. Hones. Alice looked down at her hands. *"Help her look after her money . . ."* That meant, not let her have it. How would Mrs. Hones get the money away from her? That is, if it really happened.

But it couldn't happen, She just couldn't stay in this strange place and do all those hard things she didn't know how to do.

"Well, all right then, fine, we'll expect her. In two weeks. Or perhaps even sooner. She could move in and start training before her birthday without breaking any rules."

"No," said Alice.

"Oh—they're having a party for her at the Home," Mrs. Hones explained. "Besides, any sooner would be just a bit too sudden. Alice always needs time to get used to new plans."

"All right, two weeks," said Mr. Bell. "Mrs. Leaming, why don't you show Alice around the place, where she'll be sleeping and all."

When Mrs. Leaming walked out ahead of them, Alice noticed that though she was only a little bit fat on top, she got heavier and heavier as she went down, so that her feet turned out like frogs' feet under the weight.

14

"Well," said Mrs. Hones, when they were out of the office, the door shut behind them, "that was easy! You must be hard up for help around here."

"Oh, we are; they just won't stay," said Mrs. Leaming. Then she folded her lips tight and lifted her eyebrows at Mrs. Hones, with a little tilt of her head toward Alice. "But, however, it's not really so bad. Now I'll show you the sights, Alice! Over there's the beauty shop."

"Beauty shop!" exclaimed Alice. "What do they want with that?"

An old lady was sitting on a chair in front of a sink with half her hair done up in rollers, pink scalp between.

"Aw, honey, they want it as bad as the rest of us!" said the woman who was doing the work. She was a very black-eyed, black-haired woman with a lot of make-up on. "And don't talk like that in front of them; good thing this one is deaf. Hey, you're the new aide, aren't you?"

"Word sure gets around," said Mrs. Hones.

"Is she Eye-talian?" Alice asked as they went on.

Mrs. Leaming winked at her and said. "Shrewd." She and Mrs. Hones laughed. Then Mrs. Leaming gravely said to Alice, "Maria is very good-hearted. She does crafts, too. Loves everybody. Of course, she hasn't any training."

"Poor thing," said Mrs. Hones.

Alice looked at Mrs. Leaming to see if she knew that Mrs. Hones was making fun of her. She didn't seem to. Maybe Alice noticed that quicker than a smart person like Mrs. Leaming, because it happened to her pretty often.

"Let's take the elevator. I hate steps," said Mrs. Leaming. "Though of course, I have the keys to the staircase."

15

She jingled a big bunch that hung from her belt. "I have to keep my eye on them. Even the aides and the orderlies have to get permission to open the back stairs. Leads to the laundry, and people could just waltz out with the clean clothes without anyone's seeing them."

The elevator arrived and opened itself up. It was empty. "Pee-ew," said Mrs. Hones as they got in. It looked clean, but it smelled like a toilet.

"These orderlies, they don't keep up with things." Mrs. Leaming snorted. "We'll go to Third, show Alice her room."

The elevator opened onto a hall with a hospital-like desk. Alice was introduced to two women in uniform, but pretended not to see them, because they were staring at her.

A row of old women in chairs facing the elevator also stared at her. An old man came stumping toward Alice as fast as he could come, but Mrs. Leaming waddled in between, cutting him off.

"Morning, Charlie," she said in her pleasant voice. "How are you today?"

"I'm . . . going . . . out," said Charlie, leaving wide spaces between his words. "I'm . . . going . . . home. My . . . daughter's . . . coming . . . after . . . me."

"That's right. Pretty soon," Mrs. Leaming agreed, edging Alice along on the other side of her.

"But I want to see the girl. Pretty girl," said Charlie, talking faster, trying to get past.

"Not now, Charlie. The girl has to go down the hall with me," said Mrs. Leaming.

Alice looked back. He was standing there with his hand stretched out after them. She felt sorry for him, he looked so disappointed, and after all he had thought her pretty. But she was glad they hadn't let him touch her. "When is his daughter coming?"

"Never. She's never coming," said Mrs. Leaming.

"What's that noise?" Alice asked nervously. It was a kind of despairing grunt, over and over again: "Ugh! . . . Ugh! . . . Ugh!"

"Oh, that's just Miss Carroll. She has spells of refusing her tranquilizer, and then she goes off like that. Well, here's your room, dear."

As they came to the door, it opened, and a young black girl started to come out. She stopped short, stared at Alice, and said, "Oh, no, you don't! You were planning to move the loony in on me, weren't you? Oh, no, you don't!"

"Why Appolonia, what are you saying!" said Mrs. Leaming. "You're being so rude!"

"What's rude got to do with it? In a jungle like this, you got to defend yourself."

Jungle! Yes! This girl looked like someone out of a jungle, very dark, with a great curved nose and flashing eyes. Her neat white uniform didn't tame her down at all.

And there she was, looking down on Alice!

Alice came into words. "I wouldn't room with a fucking black ass like you for a million dollars!"

2

THE PARTY at the home was no good. They had parties like this just because they had to, and nobody had any fun. Why did they do it? Alice got so deep in this problem that she was embarrassed to discover suddenly that she was still there, sitting in the place of honor at the head table, which had been decorated with crepe paper streamers and candles that they couldn't light for fear of fire.

And everyone was staring at her, evidently because Dr. Boone, who was standing up and making a speech, had just said something about her.

"So it's not just a birthday," he was saying, "but also a farewell, to one of our most charming girls."

The faces staring at her looked the same as ever: little Morgana's, shy but hopeful; Barbara Beam's, frowning and mad; the others all stages between. Mike started to clap, but nobody followed her lead, so after a few spatters, she quit.

"So now, Alice, in spite of our regret, we must say fare thee well, and godspeed as you go on to a larger life." Dr. Boone, after having waited in vain for the clapping to take hold, picked up his speech as if it were a wet glove. "But to make sure you will never forget us, as we shall never forget you, we want to give you this little remembrance, which we hope will be useful and give you pleasure."

The girls' expressions livened up a little, and they craned their necks to see what the present was. But Alice didn't even care. It was like the goodbyes, cutting the ground out from under her. She took the beautifully wrapped box and began to claw at the green and gold ribbon.

She knew she should stand up and say something. But all she could think of to say was that she wasn't leaving. This was what she had been trying to tell somebody ever since the visit to the nursing home, but there had never been a chance.

She hadn't been able to do anything right after her fight with Appolonia, because Mrs. Leaming and Mrs. Hones were so busy fixing things up—"Girls! Girls!" "Neither of you means what she said." "Never mind, we'll arrange everything. You won't have to room together."—and getting her bundled out of the place before Mr. Bell heard about it. Alice never had a chance to get a word in edge· wise. She seldom did; her words didn't come out in time unless she was simply furious, as she had been when Ap· polonia called her a loony. She'd been called that plenty of times before, but she didn't intend to have it go on, now that (as everybody told her) she was grown-up.

As she struggled with the ribbons, Alice heard a little sprinkle of laughter around her and caught the words Dr. Boone was speaking while he watched her efforts.

". . . most charming and most unpredictable—we never

know what she'll do next," he said. "We have never been able to open the package that is Alice, any more than she is able to open her gift right now."

It was the teachers and the cottage mothers who were laughing. The girls' faces were as blank as her own felt, as she divided her attention only slightly from her task, to figure out what Dr. Boone was talking about. "Charming"— that was silly. Movie stars were charming. "Unpredictable" —well, she never knew herself what she was going to do next, why should they? She was happy sometimes when she had no call to be, and other times sad, like now, when they were trying to butter her up.

And here she was, in a daze, trying to take these ribbons off, even though she knew that if she once looked at the present they were giving her it would be too late—like you couldn't take back shoes to the shoe store once you had walked in them.

But how could she stop unwrapping? Everybody was waiting. Besides, she was getting curious. It was a bigger box than she had expected.

She lifted up the lid, as she was doomed to do, and looked inside. She could see nothing but tissue paper, smoothed over and tucked down around something soft and bulky. But the tissue paper was yellow, smooth, gentle, but bright, reminding her of the changes she had seen outdoors hovering over the parkway. She folded back the paper.

The present was a sweater, a green sweater; surrounded by the yellow, it made her think of daffodils. It was a knitted sweater, with patterns winding in and out; a luxurious, expensive-looking sweater. It was beautiful.

"To set off your blonde hair," said Dr. Boone.

That was the second time! Somebody talking about her hair again, which had never happened before in her whole life.

"Alice, say thank you!" Mike was whispering into her ear.

Alice sent a blind look around the room. "Thank you," she muttered.

But she was still thinking about the blonde hair; that meant the same as golden. And the old lady in the nursing home hadn't *had* to say it.

Afterward, of course, when everybody had taken the sweater out of the box and pawed over it and looked inside the collar and read the label, "Made in Hong Kong," and said, "Well, they really make them cheap over there," it changed the sweater a little, made it seem a little duller, almost dingy. Alice tried to fold it back neatly in the paper, to protect it. But she couldn't get it to lie down.

"You can wear it with your white dress," said Morgana.

Then Morgana dropped her eyes, getting all shy, as usual, and Alice wondered if she was blushing. After Appolonia, Morgana seemed not just Colored, but nice. But it was too late to find that out.

It was too late for anything. Too late to make a fuss or to hope things would stop pushing Alice straight out into that dangerous world where so much would be expected of her. To those awful old people, those repulsive jobs, and Appolonia, who looked as if she might scratch a person's eyes out without thinking twice.

The remaining days went by. Alice skipped classes and

did her jobs badly, and nobody seemed to care. Graduation day came, and Alice followed Sheila up on the platform and got her diploma and came down, and Morgana followed her; and when everybody had done it, people clapped, and they sang the school song, and it was over. Everybody went to the dining room for refreshments with their families and friends.

"Somebody's waiting for you in the parlor," said Mike.

"Who?" asked Alice quickly. She didn't think Carol and Ernie would have come. Carol didn't like her any longer, since she wasn't little and cute, and Ernie never had.

"Just your father," said Mike.

Alice made her way through the crowds and upstairs to the parlor.

"Saw you graduate," Dad mumbled.

You could tell he didn't think graduating mattered. That was what Alice had thought, too.

"Here's some things from the kids." He handed her a box of candy and a couple of magazines. "They said to say hello."

Alice took the things and said nothing.

"Carol's still waiting tables at the Harp and Pipe," he said. "But she's taking more of them dancing lessons and picks up jobs in night spots once in a while. Ernie's doing fine with his accounting class. That boy will be rich someday."

Alice still couldn't think of anything to say.

He said it was getting to be spring, and she said yes, and then there was silence. It was like other visits, only he seemed more nervous than usual, and that made her uneasy, too. She was relieved when he stood up.

He shook hands—he hadn't kissed her in years—and started toward the door. Then he turned around and came slowly back.

"You're sure you want to go to this nursing home—take this job?" he asked. "You could come home, you know."

Alice felt something happen inside her, like her lungs collapsed or something. You could come home. He'd never said that before.

Even when she was in that first place and cried all the time, and then later at the Willowstream School when she threw herself on him (her mother was in the hospital by then) and begged him to take her away, he'd just looked hard and cold and miserable and shaken his head. From then on, she'd told herself, "I'll never go home, never."

But now she had the chance!

She stared at her father. How worried he looked! As if he really hadn't meant to say it; or if he had, could just barely get it out.

She wondered if Carol and Ernie had known he was going to offer. She didn't think so, or they wouldn't have sent the presents. Or maybe they hadn't sent the presents. Maybe he got them himself and pretended. But she didn't believe he would have thought to do that.

How upset Carol and Ernie would be if she took him up on it! And he would surely be sorry, himself. It would be awful.

A strange new feeling came over her. She wasn't just a helpless little girl that nobody wanted around. Somebody had offered her a job!

"I guess I better take this job," said Alice. "Jobs are

scarce, you know." She knew that last sentence was good even before she saw the faint, rare smile on his face.

Maybe he would tell Carol and Ernie, "She acted so darn independent."

But as soon as he was gone, she decided she must have been crazy. He had tried to rescue her from the awfulness ahead, and she—she'd refused to let him! And tomorrow it was going to happen!

She ran to her room, jammed the door shut with a chair, and cried and cried, paying no attention to Morgana's hesitant knocking. Crying was good while it lasted, like she was getting something done, heaving her shoulders and banging her head against the wall and clenching her fingernails into her palms.

But finally it ran out—she couldn't cry any more; and no good had come of it. Except she was so tired she fell asleep, hardly knowing when Mike climbed through the window and opened the door so Morgana could go to bed.

Mrs. Hones came to pick her up in the main lobby early in the morning. Nobody was around. Mike had said goodbye in the cottage, and the kids were all doing their chores or in class. Everything was finished, anyway; there was nothing left. But it did seem funny to walk out of the place where she'd been for five years and have it seem to close up behind her.

Mrs. Hones drove silently. When they had turned onto the parkway, she leaned back, lit a cigarette, and drove with one hand. She seemed a little different from usual—more as if she were there.

"I do hope you'll like it all right," she said. "It's not as if there were many choices waiting around for you."

"That's true, that's just what I said to my dad," said Alice, enjoying, again, her good sense. But then she caught something else from what Mrs. Hones had said. "What's wrong with this job?" She knew what she thought was wrong with it, but she hadn't expected Mrs. Hones to have any sympathy.

Mrs. Hones shrugged. "Well, you can judge for yourself. You saw the people. They're kind of sweet, but kind of hard to take sometimes. That makes the nurses get up-tight, and they take it out on the aides, and then the aides get riled up, and they take it out on the patients. Vicious circle. But never mind, I'll be around. I'm still responsible for you, and I can go to bat for you if you need me."

It was a nightmare ahead of her, all dark and threatening, surrounding her, no way out. Even that last part, "I'll go to bat for you"—suddenly, she didn't want that.

"Why are you responsible for me? I'm not a child any more."

"For various reasons, you're still a ward of the state. We're responsible because your parents gave you up to us."

"My mother gave me up," said Alice. "She didn't want me any more."

Mrs. Hones glanced at her. "Oh, I don't think that was it. She was ill and couldn't take care of you. She had tuberculosis."

"She didn't love me."

"Why do you jump to that conclusion? There are lots of reasons why parents feel others might care for their children better than they. Sometimes it's just because they love them so much."

25

"That doesn't make sense," said Alice. "What's the name of this street?" She didn't want to talk about it any more.

"Saw Mill River Parkway. Anyway, you remember, I gave you my phone number. If you have any trouble, let me know."

"You mean with Appolonia? I'm not going to room with her, am I?"

"No. But actually, Appolonia's not so bad."

"She sure bad-mouthed me," muttered Alice.

"Well, what about you?"

"Oh, I didn't mean anything."

"Maybe she didn't, either."

Alice thought, You're both Colored. But she didn't say it. She knew better.

They turned into the drive in front of the nursing home, and Alice saw that there were tiny little folded leaves, like little green bugs, all over the bushes.

Mrs. Leaming looked up from her desk as they came in. "Good morning, Libby, Alice. Glad to see you so bright and early. I'll take you right up to Second Floor, Alice. They're short-handed today."

Mrs. Hones had started back toward the door, but now she turned back. "You're starting her on Second?"

"That's where we need her," said Mrs. Leaming. " 'Bye, Libby. Take your suitcase, Alice, and after I've introduced you to the charge nurse on Second, you can go to your room and change."

Mrs. Hones was still standing there. "Who's she rooming with?"

"Francine Peters, a very sweet girl. She's a field worker from Columbia School of Social Work."

"And living in? Must be a masochist. Well, bye-bye, Alice. I'll be seeing you. Remember my phone number . . . Bye-bye," she said again.

Alice felt like running after her, as she finally went out. Mrs. Hones had been her social worker for five years. They didn't like each other—but they knew each other.

Now she had only this stranger, Mrs. Leaming. But at any rate, she smiled oftener than Mrs. Hones. "Come along, now," she said pleasantly.

She was, at least, a fellow white-person. "Where is—will I see Appolonia?" Alice asked.

Mrs. Leaming laughed gently. "Oh, she's somewhere around. Don't worry about her. Her bark's worse than her bite." She started walking fatly into the elevator.

"Does Appolonia work on Second?"

"Not right now, she doesn't. She's doing a special job, training with the podiatrist—the foot doctor—so she can be his assistant. You won't see much of her for a while."

Thank goodness.

The trip to Second Floor was all too short. The door opened upon the same kind of hall and desk she had seen on Third Floor. Only now there was no Mrs. Hones behind her, no home to go back to, no escape.

A middle-aged nurse with a little cap on top was writing busily on a chart. "Is this the new girl?" she asked, hardly looking up from her work. "Pan! Pan! Come here at once."

Alice looked confidently along the hall; surely someone would come running at once in answer to that command. Nothing happened. The nurse went on writing. Finally a heavy blonde girl came strolling out of a room on the right-hand corridor.

"Well, Pan, so you finally made it," said the nurse. "This is Alice, our new helper. Alice, Pan. I'm Miss Boston, by the way. Please show her around, Pan, and introduce her."

"I haven't got the time, Miss Boston," grumbled Pan. "Don't you realize, Jane's off, and Petrie; seems like we can't even get started cleaning people up. Suzy needs this, and Mr. O'Leary needs that, and old Fezelle is all over the place."

"Please do as I say, Pan. Don't you realize this is a step in the right direction, a new aide to help you." Her voice was sharp. Mrs. Hones had said the nurses get up-tight, the aides get riled.

"Oh, all right, come along," said Pan. "Might as well take a look first at the few we've managed to get out to the sun parlor."

The large public room looked more like a schoolroom than a sun parlor. Straight chairs stood stiffly around the walls, unoccupied, while wheelchairs with old people humped over in them were drawn up in front of a TV, turned on, very blurry.

"Well, here's Mrs. Perciballi," said Pan, stopping before a little hairpin of a dark-eyed lady who was tied into her chair.

"Ah! Signorina, please! Please!" the old lady moaned, reaching out desperately toward Alice. Alice moved closer, dazed but fascinated, and the old lady seized Alice's hand in her own active claw and began kissing it noisily. Alice snatched her hand away, wiping off the saliva on her skirt.

"Come on, Perciballi, none of that," said Pan in a loud commanding tone. "Look out, Alice, don't let her grab you,

you'll never get loose. This is Mr. Beiderheim. He's a sweet old thing."

Mr. Beiderheim was a thin old man with fine clear features and papery skin blotched with brown spots. He looked into Alice's eyes and a faint smile dawned on his face. He lifted his hand in a shaky, but graceful, gesture, as if he meant to salute her.

"Here's Steiner, Plass, and Winters," said Pan, waving at each as they passed the two old women and another old man, whose watery eyes followed them indifferently. "These people in the Sun Parlor are the best on this floor! Gives you some idea. This is the floor for the most severely disabled. Bed cases, wheelchair cases, most of them senile—you know, out of it; and incontinent—don't know enough to go to the bathroom. You can tell, can't you? Pee-ew!"

As they went down the hall, the bad smell got worse. A laundry cart was picking up piles of dirty linen, dumped beside the doors. Inside the rooms old people still lay in their beds or huddled in wheelchairs, and Pan called out the names as they passed. The old people heard without understanding, and their names went right past Alice—she couldn't grasp, let alone remember them. What was the use? She would never be able to do what they wanted.

"Well, that's enough for now," said Pan, when they got back to the desk. "You can take your suitcase up, and they'll show you your room. They'll give you a uniform—change and come back and help me. I've got to get back to that horrible Mrs. Witherspoon—you hear her?"

You couldn't help hearing her. "Nurse! Nurse! Nurse! I need the bedpan! Nurse! Come at once!"

Well, thought Alice, as she went up in the elevator. *Well!* She couldn't even begin to sort out all the horrible things she'd seen. She'd just have to try to figure out some way to get out of here. She felt in her pocket to make sure she still had the slip of paper with Mrs. Hones's number.

3

THE NURSE on third floor didn't recognize her at first.

"What can I do for you? Oh, you're the new girl."

Charlie had been standing nearby, looking as though he were propped up on his own legs, watching an aide push an old lady past in a wheelchair, but when the nurse spoke, he saw Alice, and his face lighted up. He began stumping toward her as fast as he could go.

"Now, Charlie," said the nurse, coming out from behind the desk and cutting in front of him, gently swinging him around by the shoulders. "Come on, what's-your-name— oh, yes, Alice—down this way. Don't worry about Charlie. He'll get used to you and give up, pretty soon."

The room was the last one before the end door, which bore an exit sign. Alice remembered Mrs. Leaming had said the doors were all locked. The nurse knocked and then opened the door.

There was somebody in there.

It was a shock. Alice had thought her room would be someplace where she could hide.

"This is Francine," said the nurse. "Francine, your new roommate—what's your name again, dear?"

"Ah, Alice! At last!" said Francine.

Alice didn't like the nurse forgetting her name, nor Francine knowing it so well. She leaned against the door, feeling weak, pinned there by the gaze of the other girl.

Lounging there at ease in her desk chair, eyeing Alice with bright dark eyes, a smile playing over her lips—oh, this one was different! Even her clothes—like a model. The aide's uniform that looked like a potato sack on Pan looked like some special new style on her.

"Don't be scared! (I'm not *scared*, Alice thought indignantly.) I'm looking forward to getting acquainted with you. I'm sure we're going to get along fine."

Alice didn't know about that. Of all the girls she'd roomed with, she'd gotten along best with Morgana, by acting as if she wasn't there.

"Are you going to unpack?"

"When I'm ready," muttered Alice. What was the use of unpacking when she was going to leave?

"Want me to help?"

"No way," said Alice.

Francine laughed a little. "Oh well, OK." She got up and threw open the closet door. "See, I saved this half for you. These are your hangers."

Part of the closet was empty, the rest stuffed with matching garment bags.

"You don't look like you belonged here," Alice said abruptly. "How come?"

Francine laughed pleasantly. "I know what you mean," she said. "Well, it's sort of a field trip for me. I'm studying

32

for my Master's in Social Work, and I'm specializing in Geriatrics."

"In *what?*" asked Alice.

"Geriatrics. It's a long word, but it just means a study of old people," said Francine. "Now, tell me about yourself." She leaned forward, her hands loosely folded around her knees, smiling invitingly.

"Why, you thinking about studying me, too?" asked Alice. "Some other time. I got to get back on the floor."

"Don't you have to put on your uniform, first?" asked Francine.

Alice put it on fast and left without saying goodbye. She was proud of her phrase "got to get back on the floor."

But by the time she reached the elevator, she felt all oozed down into her shoes, because she didn't *want* to get back on the floor.

But when Charlie saw her and ambled out to get her, she just put up a warning hand, like a red light, and he stopped in his tracks. She was startled. How easily she had controlled him! The disappointment in his eyes was like a child's; even that she was glad about.

On Second, Pan was lounging against the desk talking to the nurse. "Oh, here you are. Come along with me now and watch what I do."

Pan strutted off down the hall, not even looking back to see if Alice was following.

The nurse called after them, "Now, Alice, don't watch everything she does!" and laughed. Pan just gave a smart-alecky wave back over her shoulder.

A short handsome black boy came along pushing a dry mop.

"Bon jour, mon ami," said Pan.

A foreign language. Like in a song. The black boy smiled, and threw back at Pan a whole bunch of soft words like little dustrags.

"Oh, go along with you, Jacques," said Pan. "This is Alice."

"Enchantée." But he was still looking at Pan with those soft smiling eyes.

That was how it went. Everybody they met had a word for Pan, and she always had one to toss back. Alice had no words. Nor was there any reason for her to need any. No one looked at her.

They met nurses, aides, orderlies. She couldn't remember them all. They were all different, but they all had in common a kind of coiled energy, ready and dangerous. They all knew what it was all about, their bright eyes knowing, their bright tongues loose (as Alice remembered Mama saying about Carol) at both ends.

Alice was afraid of all of them, but especially the orderlies. They were so strong. Even though they merely sauntered along, kidding with Pan, lazy and easygoing, you could feel their strength from looking at their muscles. When they mopped, they used large, sweeping motions, and when they lifted an old person into wheelchair or bed, their arms bulged, and their legs were braced, but they transferred their burdens like feathers.

Alice had hardly seen boys at all since she'd left the Willowstream place, when she was—let's see—eleven. But she'd heard about them. They were scary. They could hurt you. But the girls here didn't act afraid of them at all.

Though the aides were girls, like herself, they were altogether different. They knew what was what. All Alice knew was what she saw happening, and it didn't seem to make sense.

She thought the nurses were far above everyone else, with their starchy skirts and funny little hats, and sweaters swinging from their shoulders. They thought and wrote and gave orders, instead of rushing about and working and complaining. But the aides and orderlies made fun of them and laughed behind their backs.

As for the patients, Alice tried not to notice the patients at all. She didn't want even to look at them, let alone touch them—the foggy, repulsive, rickety creatures. They seemed all alike. Their coarse, wrinkled skin and dull, vacant eyes repelled her. Unbearable.

Pan took her down to dinner, which was eaten with the other aides in the basement, next to the kitchen. Most of them had met her already, which was all they seemed to need to do about her. They chattered and laughed while Alice ate hot dogs and beans. Pan paid no attention when the meal was over, going off without a backward look, so Alice went to her room, and then she went to bed, because there was nothing else to do. She lay there wondering when she would quit, and how.

She didn't know how long she had slept when a bright slit cut through the dark and a gentle click broke the silence. She opened her eyes to the sight of Francine turning on the bed lamp. It was like a picture from a magazine: the smooth dark bell of hair falling forward as Francine bent, and swinging back as she rose.

"Oh, you're awake!" said Francine. "I hope I didn't disturb you."

Alice shook her head on the pillow. No. It was not disturbing. It was nice to wake up and see such a pleasant sight, as if this were the rule of things—quiet movement, considerate voice, friendly smile.

Her whole feeling about Francine turned around. How lucky she was to be rooming with Francine! Maybe she could even tell Francine about wanting to leave and find out how to do it.

"The first day in a new job is always hard, I'm sure you must be terribly tired," said Francine.

Oh, yes! Alice searched for words to tell how hard, how tired.

Francine had turned her back and was undressing. She slipped a lovely blue nightie over her head, then put on a white robe.

"Tell you what, I'll do my studying downstairs tonight so you can rest. Another night when you're not so tired we'll talk and get acquainted.

She switched off the lamp and was gone, like a dream; had she really been there?

Not really, Alice thought, empty with disappointment.

The next day was a nightmare. Alice followed Pan about like a can tied to a car with a string; she didn't know what was going on, and Pan didn't tell her. Alice didn't have time even to wonder what to do next, just tried desperately to keep from being noticed.

She went to bed early again, but waited in the dark, awake, for Francine.

When the slit of light, the soft sounds, the glowing flower of the lampshade happened again, she said, even before

Francine had glanced over to see if she was asleep, "When is the school?"

Francine looked at her for a minute, her head on one side, and a smile on one side, too. "School?"

"Mr. Bell said—I could learn about—well, what I have to do—"

Francine gave a little whistle. "Oh, that's what he said, is it? In-training, that's what he said, isn't it? Well, Alice, alas, that was all bull. What you learn, you have to pick up on the job. Ask questions. Watch. It isn't so complicated. By no means. You'll gradually get to understand."

As she undressed, the same way she had the night before, Alice saw her shake her head and heard a ghostly little chuckle.

I'll ask her how to quit, thought Alice. As soon as she gets into bed and turns off the light.

But Francine didn't get into bed. She did turn off the light.

"Still got a lot of studying," she said. "See you later."

Alice turned over and wondered how she was going to stand it another day to not quit and not know what to do.

She did stand it another day, and another, and another, pretending not to be there, except when she was running errands for Pan and doing nasty little jobs like carrying dirty linen and emptying bedpans and mopping up wet places.

But on the fifth day when she got to the desk, Pan was not there.

Miss Boston looked up from her records. "Oh, Alice! Am I glad to see you. This is Pan's day off. Would you just go around and check on everybody, the way she always does, and take care of any urgent needs before we start on the clean-up?"

Alice thought in panic, "I'll quit now."

But Miss Boston had gone back to her records. After hesitating a moment, Alice walked down the hall.

She was stopped by a thin old lady. Suzy, Alice realized. She hadn't known she knew the name of this thin little old person, but now she saw that she did know it, and also knew what Suzy was going to do next. She was, of course, very old, but she was girlish, too, slim and flexible, with large questioning eyes, and her hair hanging down her back in a skimpy gray braid. She began to walk toward Alice, with an eager expression on her face.

But she wouldn't make sense, Alice knew that, and started to get away from her. But there was something worse than Suzy the other way. This was Mr. Fezelle, who was French. He said he was French. If anyone said he wasn't French, there was hell to pay. But the worst thing about Mr. Fezelle, from the girls' point of view, was that he messed around, and he was sprier than Charlie and harder to keep away from.

So instead of escaping from Suzy, Alice decided to escape from Mr. Fezelle. She went right up to Suzy, and said, "How are you today?"

Suzy's wide, vague eyes looked pleased. "Where?" she asked, putting out one hand pleadingly. "Where that day yet?" Or at least, that was what it sounded like.

"Right over there," said Alice, because she had to say something.

Suzy looked anxious, but hopeful. "Try not the way?"

Pan had told Alice that Suzy couldn't say the right word

38

for what she meant. How awful that must be, Alice thought, looking at her more closely, really thinking about her. Did Suzy know what she wanted to say? Did she know she didn't really say it? How awful. If you couldn't even say the words.

"Sure," said Alice, and patted Suzy. She hadn't patted any of them before. In fact, she'd never patted anyone.

Suzy smiled!

Next came the room of Mrs. Tree and Mrs. Adams. Mrs. Tree was grotesque. She insisted on wearing powder and rouge smeared thickly all over her network of wrinkles, lipstick on her shapeless lips.

"Hello, Mrs. Tree," said Alice, as Pan always did. "Need anything today?"

And as Mrs. Tree looked up dumbly out of her circus-clown face, Alice felt something move inside her, like crying, and said unexpectedly, "You look nice!"

It was such a lie that Alice was scared when she heard herself say it. But Mrs. Tree's face creased in smile-wrinkles, and she gave a little bob of her head. "You'll make me proud!" she said quaveringly.

Alice had thought she wouldn't understand, but she did.

"OK," said Alice, and went on to Mrs. Adams.

These two women sat opposite each other, twelve feet apart, all day long, each looking out her own window, never speaking. Not that they were enemies, they just didn't know each other, Pan said.

"Do you need anything, Mrs. Adams?"

Mrs. Adams turned her delicate face from the window. "Did you notice that leaves are unfolding on the bushes? Lovely, isn't it! Spring at last."

"I saw a robin the other day," said Alice.

39

But Mrs. Adams turned away again. She never answered anyone. Alice had been deceived at first by her ladylike appearance, and asked Pan about her.

"She's all right, isn't she?"

"Don't know her hand from her foot."

So you never could tell. Alice looked to see if the floor was dry under Mrs. Adams—often it wasn't—and checked the water in the pitchers.

In the next room, Mr. Wheeler was waiting for her. He wasn't stupid. "Nurse, nurse," he gasped as Alice came in. "Help me, little girl, I'm out of breath, I'm dying. Get me the oxygen."

"I'll tell Miss Boston," said Alice. He wasn't really dying, that is, not just this minute. His lungs were gone, Pan said, so he could just manage to gulp in enough air to keep alive. There was an oxygen tank, but it was just for emergencies, but it made him feel wonderful, so he had an emergency whenever anyone went by.

Alice cast an eye over at Mr. Burket, who was reading *The New York Times.* He had been reading last Sunday's edition all week. He tried to keep all the old ones in a pile by his bed, but Pan said Nurse Boston took them away every once in a while; old papers attract roaches.

Mr. Burket must be very smart, Alice thought. He was on Second not because he was senile, but because he was heavy duty. His foot was all rotted out with ulcers and had to be dressed every day, bandaged, padded, and elevated on a footstool.

"Need anything, Mr. Burket?"

"Just a drop of Irish whiskey!"

"I don't think . . ." said Alice doubtfully, for he'd never

40

brought this up when she came with Pan; and Mr. Burket interrupted her by laughing, a papery breathless laugh. His eyes wrinkled into slits, his mouth gaped over his toothless gums (his false teeth stood in a glass on the bed-table) and his big leathery nose stood out further than ever.

"Don't fear, little girl, I know you can't get it for me. Just a—well, a sort of a joke between friends, understand?"

Alice stared, then nodded, but by then he had gone back to his paper. What did he find there that was so interesting? He seemed to go into it and close the door.

"Nurse! Nurse!" It was Mrs. Lindley. Alice put her head in the door and said, "You ready to come off the pan?" (That was what Pan always said.)

Mrs. Lindley, a very light Colored lady, like caramel ice cream, nodded and dimpled. Alice hadn't taken anybody off the pan by herself. She was nervous, but managed to lift the light old body, wipe the delicate slack skin, and remove the smelly sloshing pan from under her without spilling. Then she threw a towel over the pan in the proper manner.

"You want to go to the sun parlor today?"

Mrs. Lindley dimpled and shook her head. "No, I guess not today, dear. My niece might come today, and she wouldn't know where to find me."

Alice already knew that Mrs. Lindley was wrong about this. Pan said the niece did come once in a great while, but of course if she did she would be able to find Mrs. Lindley in the sun parlor. Mrs. Lindley just didn't want to go to the sun parlor, but she was too nice to say no.

Alice had to go there now, herself, and see how the sun parlor regulars were getting along. She dreaded Mrs. Perciballi.

But before she could get there, another interruption.

"Nurse! Nurse!"

It was Mrs. Witherspoon, who roomed with Mrs. Symes.

"Where have you been? I was calling and calling. Would you please straighten my pillow?"

She was a very heavy woman, so it was hard to unearth the pillow from where it had slipped down behind her in the wheelchair, and after shaking it up, to settle it back comfortably behind her.

"No, no, not like that. Higher. Higher."

Alice struggled with the pillow.

"Oh, my, you're so clumsy. Now you've got it too high. And when you've finished with that, I need my socks changed. The ones I have on always slide down and cause me untold agony. And then you can clip my nails."

"I'm not allowed to cut your nails," said Alice, kneeling to take off the socks. (Pan had told her, "Only the podiatrist can cut nails.")

She found the clean socks in a drawer and took off the offensive ones. How awful! The hornlike toenails curved clear under the ends of the toes! And this was what Appolonia was learning to take care of! It served her right.

"Oh! Oh! You're hurting me! Stop that you bad wicked girl! Can't you be a little bit careful?"

It was like trying to fit a clenched iron fist into a glove.

"The people they hire in this home!" moaned Mrs. Witherspoon. "Ignorant blacks and imbeciles! I'm going to write to the governor!"

You couldn't hit the patients. Alice had never thought she would want to and had been shocked when Pan was occasionally cross with them. Now she understood. She wanted to hit Mrs. Witherspoon. She got up and walked away, leaving the second sock on the floor.

She was startled to see Jacques in the corridor. He was laughing and had evidently seen what happened. *"Bon! Bon!"* he exclaimed, and seeing she didn't understand the word, he clasped his hands and lifted them in the air, in a gesture she knew must be approving.

Wondering, Alice walked on to the sun parlor. Mrs. Perciballi saw her at once and began to cry and moan.

To put off the necessity of getting into Mrs. Perciballi's reach, Alice stopped by Mr. Beiderheim.

"How are you?" she asked.

She got no answer. She had expected none. He never spoke to anyone. But he continued to look at her steadily, as he always did. And suddenly there came a little muffled sound. Alice looked down and saw that Mr. Beiderheim was trying to say something. His hands trembled on the chair-arms; a faint color showed in his bone-white face.

"I—I want you to know," said Mr. Beiderheim's thin husk of a voice, "that I think you're very nice. You are pretty, like my wife when she was young, when she was just fifteen, and we married, in Germany."

Alice's heart seemed to give a big flop. She couldn't think of anything to say, but she patted Mr. Beiderheim's arm. That was the second person she had patted.

The she saw Mr. Fezelle peering around the door. He looked like a wicked dark gnome in a fairy tale. He had seen her pat Mr. Beiderheim. Like the wicked dark gnome he came lurching in, lifted up his cane, and started beating Mr. Beiderheim.

What should she do! She had to do something. Alice got

hold of Mr. Fezelle's shoulder and pulled as hard as she could. Mrs. Perciballi started screaming, and Nurse Boston came to the door, screamed herself, and in a moment Jaques dashed in. All this time Alice was hanging onto Mr. Fezelle with all her strength, but he was still beating Mr. Beiderheim with his stick. Mr. Beiderheim's forehead was bleeding.

Jacques grabbed Mr. Fezelle and pulled him off, and Miss Boston leaned over Mr. Beiderheim, while Alice sank down on the bed. Then the ambulance came—she could hear it shrieking.

At lunch, that was all anybody talked about. Other mealtimes they had gossiped and chattered in twos or threes, leaving Alice out, of course; but today she was the center of it.

"Poor old Beiderheim, he was useless, but never did anybody any harm. Why'd Fezelle go after him, Alice?"

Alice couldn't explain, but she did say something. She cleared her throat and said, "Will he get well?"

"Probably not. One less," said Billy Lass. "And I sure hope they send Fezelle to psychiatric—have to, after this."

When Pan came to dinner that night, back from her day off, she said, "Gee, Alice! Three cheers for you. You got rid of two of my patients at one fell swoop! What did you think when he started to come?"

"I thought he might kill Mr. Beiderheim," said Alice. "He lifted his cane and his eyes flashed, just like the devil."

She thought this sounded good, but Francine, across the table, looked indignant.

"Oh, come on, that poor old man! He didn't know what he was doing. You have to keep in mind, always, that they're

44

not in control anymore. You must try, Alice, to be grown-up about it."

Jacques, who was sitting next to Francine, began to laugh. "Oh, she grown-up all right! Alice grown up enough to walk out on Witherspoon when she act up today!"

Everybody laughed, and had to hear that story, too; and Alice felt as if they were laughing more at Francine than at her.

4

ALICE tossed and turned in her bed.

She kept seeing again Mr. Fezelle's furious face as he came toward her with his stick upraised. She saw the blood on Mr. Beiderheim's head.

The talk at the table went over and over in her mind. *Oh come on, that poor old man . . . You must try to be grown-up Alice . . .* And then, Jacques: *She grown-up enough to walk out on Witherspoon today!*

When Francine came in tonight, she had pretended Alice wasn't there and gone out immediately after she'd changed, skipping her usual speech about having to study and getting to know each other.

She hadn't meant all that stuff anyway; probably would be glad if Alice would quit and get the hell out of there.

"Don't worry, I'm going to get the hell out of here," Alice would say. "You don't have to bother about me anymore."

But on the other hand, why should she get the hell out of here? She had gone all through the rounds today and done all the things Pan always did and protected Mr. Beiderheim and walked out on Mrs. Witherspoon besides! She'd never done so much in one day before in her life.

In fact, when morning came she was sorry she was going to have to follow Pan around, after being on her own.

Pan stopped at the desk, as usual, to gossip with the nurse before starting out, and Alice went on alone.

"What are you reading about?" she asked Mr. Burket.

Mr. Burket put down his paper and looked at her. Then his slow smile covered his face, taking over the eyes and making his mouth sink in further than ever.

"What am I reading about? Lots of things," he said. "I read more than they put in this paper. Take for instance. Here's a article about"—he hunted up the place laboriously, then slowly sounded out the word, just as Alice would have done—"Tan-zan-i-a. I ain't never heard of that place before, but when I read down the column a ways, I find out it's nothing but old Tanganyika, where I helped unload a cargo back in nineteen-ought-nine."

"You've been there!" said Alice. This old man sitting in the chair with his foot on a stool! Impossible!

"I signed on as cabin boy in a sailing ship out of Southampton in nineteen-ought-three."

Then he didn't say anything more, and Alice saw that he had fallen asleep.

Pan came in. "Hey, you're behind. Finish the beds quick."

Mr. Burket woke up. ". . . but they tried to put me in jail, for my age. I was only thirteen. So I stowed away in a clipper bound for China."

Pan shook her finger at him. "Oh, come, come, Mr. Burket. I don't believe a word of it. Don't waste time listening to his stories, Alice."

"Right," said Alice. ("Right" was all she ever said to

47

Pan.) But she waited till Pan had gone on, turned back and said to Mr. Burket, "You can tell me the rest tomorrow."

"What's that?" said Mr. Burket. He had gone back to the *New York Times.*

Alice went on and made beds as fast as she could, paying no attention to Mrs. Witherspoon's complaints, but she ran into Pan again in Mrs. Tree's room.

"Here she is!" Mrs. Tree called out, though Pan was just pulling a clean dress over her head. "Here's the pretty girl!"

"What do you mean, here's the pretty girl?" demanded Pan. "You used to call me that!"

"Oh, but she's prettier than you!" said Mrs. Tree, drawing out her syllables very long and rolling her eyes.

This was no place to say, "Right!" Alice didn't want Pan to get mad at her, so she said, "That's just because I tell her *she's* pretty."

"Yuk," said Pan.

Alice decided not to talk to patients much when Pan was around. She couldn't afford to have Pan mad at her. But she knew Pan didn't mind much what anybody did, so long as it didn't hit her in the face. Pan was going to quit and get married in the fall; she was just working to get money for clothes for her wedding.

Things kept pretty quiet the next few days. Alice had lived through it, knew what to expect. She submitted to Pan, walled out Francine, and avoided Billy Lass Holder, who lived next door and tried too hard to be friendly. Alice had the feeling she couldn't be trusted. Though why she didn't know. She pretended the orderlies weren't alive; except she rather enjoyed watching (while pretending not to notice) the games they played with the aides—kind of like a movie. Only not ending. Not coming out either right or wrong, just changing all the time. She did like Jacques, who had stood up for her; and she admired Petrie Flynn, but feared him. He was gentle with the old men, but he was bold and loud and black. A guy called Browny was at the bottom, in her judgment. The others moved up and down.

She watched out for Appolonia, but seldom saw her. When she did, Alice felt apprehensive—also interested. There was something different about Appolonia, as there was (in another way) about Francine. They seemed to know what they were doing. Appolonia was always going somewhere, or else coming back. She hurried in late to meals and turned off people's questions with smart-aleck answers, then hurried out again to her special work, as if it were very important.

Alice was beginning to have special work, too. She was sent down to Therapy one day with Ann Johnson.

"Be very careful with her," said Nurse Bishop, as Pan brought Ann down the hall in a wheelchair. "Remember, she's ninety-eight. She's fragile, and besides, she might run away."

Alice looked at Miss Johnson and didn't believe it. She believed Miss Johnson was ninety-eight, but she didn't believe Miss Johnson would run away. How could she! Alice looked at the nurse with her doubt showing.

"Yes, yes, I know she's a very old lady, and that she seems perfectly rational, but she does have one big obsession. Why do you think we keep her on Second in the first place? She may be ninety-eight, but she's smarter than most of us, and I mean patient or staff. But she does try to get out. They caught her once in the driveway, racing her wheelchair as if she were riding a horse."

"Good morning, dear," said Miss Johnson when Pan turned her over to Alice. "So we're going to have a little outing together, you and I!"

"See?" Pan murmured to Alice. "She's trying to snow you. Take care." And she pinched Alice's arm slightly to emphasize her warning.

Alice jerked her arm away and rolled the wheelchair into the elevator.

"I must say, I'm glad to escape that atmosphere of death and decay, otherwise known as Second Floor," said Miss Johnson when the door had slid shut and the elevator had begun its noiseless descent. "Poor old things. I'm sorry for them, I even likc some of them, but they are depressing." She cocked her head sideways to look up at Alice over her shoulder. "How can you stand us, when you're so young?"

"I'm not that young," said Alice. She knew she didn't mean exactly that. She meant, I'm not that undepressing. But Miss Johnson took the remark at face value. She laughed quite hard, even though she was so thin and blue-veined and shaky.

"Of course you're not, nobody ever is," she said. "I can remember feeling absolutely antedeluvian when I was eighteen. I suppose you are eighteen, aren't you?"

Then the door slid open, and they were in the basement, opposite the open door to the therapy room.

Therapy began at ten every morning, and again at two every afternoon. Alice had been shown around the "department" (one room) during her first week. There were bars

50

attached to the walls, bars suspended horizontally across the floor, stair steps going up and then down without having been anywhere, and other contraptions. There was a man with thin curly black hair, called Mr. Pitz, who was in charge, and orderlies supported the patients as they moved tremblingly in and out of the bars or up and down the steps.

"Good morning, Miss Johnson! How glorious! You've made my day by coming down," said Mr. Pitz, bounding to meet them.

"Go away with you," said Miss Johnson. "You're a flatterer, and a flatterer is up to no good. My father told me to watch out for gentlemen like you—alas! That's why I'm single to this day."

"To this day, but no further," said Mr. Pitz. "Now you've done it, you've given me the signal. Miss Johnson, will you marry me?"

All the times these jokes were going on, Mr. Pitz was lifting Miss Johnson carefully out of her wheelchair and helping her gently over the slightly raised threshold into the practic room.

Alice had been told to leave Miss Johnson there and return for her at eleven. She went back to the elevator and pressed the button to call it back.

"Hi! I say! Girl! Turn around here!"

She heard the voice, and heard it say all these things, before she realized it could be talking to her. The slightly familiar tones were husky and rather loud. Alice turned around.

"There! I knew it was you! I recognized your golden hair! I wondered if you would really fall for their line and take this job."

51

The old lady was standing in the doorway, half bent over to the left, with her hand braced on her thigh.

"I'm Mrs. Daniels, remember? Only nobody calls me that. My name's Allegra, but they all call me Leg. That's funny, isn't it? Especially since I've got one game one. Come here, girl. Come here, Alice. I want to talk to you."

Alice hesitated. The elevator had come, and the door slid open, and it would only wait so long.

"Let it go. Come. Come," said the old lady commandingly.

Alice couldn't quite make up her mind; started toward the closing doors; stopped again.

She said apprehensively, "They said I should come back."

"Don't be afraid. They can wait. I wanted to explain to you what I said the first time I saw you. I'm rather abrupt, and people are sometimes afraid of me, or offended, but I'm not really a bad old girl. Did you ever hear of Longfellow?"

Alice kept her mouth shut and stared at the old lady. She couldn't catch up. The old lady waited, and finally said, "Hiawatha?"

Oh! Yes! Gitchee-gummee. *Da*-da-*da*-da-*da*-da-*da*da. She laughed, remembering the beat of the words.

"Gitchee-gummee," she said.

"Exactly!" cried the old lady. "Well, he wrote another poem—several, in fact—but one that tells about children: *The Children's Hour,* it's called. 'Grave Alice, and laughing Allegra, and Edith with golden hair.' Well, you see, that was always my line, because I was laughing Allegra. And when I heard your name was Alice, and saw your golden hair, it seemed as if you fitted right in, even if it isn't in just

52

the right order: Alice with golden hair, when in the poem it's Edith. And you are grave! But not all the time, I hope. Anyway, we're destined to be friends, don't you think? . . . Oh-oh, here's my keeper."

Alice, preventing her mouth from falling open only with effort, saw a broad young man come up in front of the old lady and put his hands gently on her shoulders.

"Yes, yes, I'll get to work now," said the old lady. "But first you must meet Alice with golden hair. Alice, this is Ginger Man. That's not his name, but that's what I call him. He's the physiotherapist."

The young man shook his head hard. He didn't seem to pay much attention to Alice and didn't speak.

"All right, assistant therapist, then," said the old lady, and allowed him to help her back into the room. After watching them go, Alice again pressed the elevator button.

Nobody on Second Floor seemed to notice she'd been slow getting back. Pan was drinking coffee with the nurse.

"Go get the laundry collected," she called to Alice. Alice hoped that when she went down at eleven to take Mr. Winters down and bring Miss Johnson back she'd see that old lady (Mrs. Daniels—*Leg?*) again, and hear more of the strange, fascinating things she said. But when she went, there was no sign of her. Miss Johnson was waiting, or rather, she was sitting there in her chair prepared to go back, but she was sound asleep, her chin sunk on her chest, her broad white forehead all that was to be seen.

Alice released the brake on the wheelchair and turned it around as gently and smoothly as she could, hoping not to wake up the old lady. She liked to see the patients sleep. It seemed to be the best time for them as it was for her. But Miss Johnson's quavery voice rose immediately.

"Good morning, dear. It is still morning, isn't it? Still morning. Strange, at my age, the years are so short and the days are so long."

They were alone in the elevator.

"You see, I worry such a lot about my niece," said Miss Johnson. "She's much worse off than I. She needs to see me. She's in the chronic ward of the hospital, just down the street. But they won't let me go down to see her."

She was asleep again by the time they reached Second Floor. Alice wheeled her quietly into her room, and later went back for Mr. Winters. But she caught no more sight of her puzzling friend, though the young man (Ginger Man) helped her get Mr. Winters into his wheelchair. He didn't say anything, though, or act as if they'd been introduced.

As she emptied bedpans and cleaned floors that afternoon, Alice wondered about the contradiction between what the nurse had said about Miss Johnson's running away, as if she were crazy, and what Miss Johnson had said about her niece needing her. Miss Johnson had to have made that up. The nurse must be right.

Still, nurses weren't always right.

Often Alice could see plainly what was going on—like lighted platforms that flashed by when you rode the subway, to be swallowed up in darkness the next moment. But she didn't know where those places were, or when she was to get off. The best she could do was try to imitate people who did know.

But what if those smart people didn't agree? Then Alice had to try to decide which one was right.

54

She had decided, for instance, when she was a little tiny girl that Daddy must be right and Mama wrong. That was because Mama always wanted to hold her, and Daddy said she should stand on her own two feet. Daddy wasn't cross, but he was worried. Being worried was right. But then Mama got worried, too, and that was wrong, that was the end. But you should never think about that.

In the home, of course, Dr. Boone had always been most right, and Mike about next; but the cooks and housekeepers were sometimes wrong, even though they were often nicer. But also, they were sometimes meaner. Cookies or swats, you couldn't tell what to expect.

And now, in this place, it must be Mr. Bell and Mrs. Leaming who were most right, and then the nurses, then the aides, and at the bottom, the patients. She didn't put the orderlies anywhere at all.

But she kept on getting confused. Though the aides were on the bottom of her list, they affected her most of all. She had to eat meals with them; and at meals they talked all the time, especially at dinner, when they had given up their burden to the night shift. There were ten aides and orderlies who lived in, and they all ate together except when somebody had enough money to go out.

How could you tell even which of them was right? They all acted different. Jacques Ben Prince, who was Haitian and knew barely enough English to get along, spoke with his bright eyes, his warm smile, his invariable willingness. Petrie was tense and angry. He came from Harlem and was going to be a doctor, and he never let them forget it.

"Don't know nothing about geriatrics, this staff," he said

that night over his second helping of chicken and dumplings.

"That's true," said Francine, who paid more attention to him than she did to anyone else. "They don't make the least use of the discoveries about Vitamin E. Nor do they even consider the system of frequent small feedings that has worked so well in a lot of small nursing homes upstate."

"Don't know nothing about that garbage," said Appolonia, flashing angrily at Francine. "And I don't know how you know, working only three hours a day, and on First Floor at that. But I sure-enough know the staff don't give a damn about the people. Do you know Mr. Bell is throwing Matilda out in the street if her kids don't pay up by next Thursday when the books have to be closed?"

This was greeted by cheers and hand claps. Matilda! Well, how can you blame him? was the general idea. Matilda was Mrs. Witherspoon.

"No," retorted Appolonia, pounding the table with her fist. "Of course she's a lousy old fool, but just the same, you shouldn't ought to treat a person like a pound of bacon!"

"A side of beef, you mean," said Petrie.

Alice said abruptly, without knowing she was going to speak, "They don't listen."

Heads turned. Alice had said nothing at meals, all this time, three weeks now, except that once.

"Who don't listen? What do you mean, Alice?" asked Pan.

"*They* don't—to the patients. The *nurses*," said Alice, impatient because they didn't understand.

"That's true, of course, but look who's talking," said Appolonia.

56

"Well, *look!*" said Alice in her mad tone. "Miss Johnson. She isn't really just running away, she wants to visit her niece."

"Oh, nuts," said Pan. "I don't think she even has a niece."

"She does, too," muttered Alice.

But it shook her to have Pan so positive. Pan must know more than Alice about what was what.

But Alice still liked Miss Johnson and managed to be there at the right time to take her down to Therapy.

"Well, my dear, how are you this lovely day? Did you notice the look of spring this morning! Perhaps we could stop off at First Floor and just go out long enough for a breath of air!"

It sounded nice, but Alice knew she'd better play it carefully. "Guess we ought to go on down. They're expecting you."

But when they reached the basement, the usual air of busy confusion was missing. A few patients sat in the hall in wheelchairs, or on the plastic chairs provided for ambulatory patients. Mrs. Daniels was one of these.

"Ah! So they goofed on your floor, too," said Mrs. Daniels cheerfully. "Seems Mr. Pitz sent word that he and Ginger Man would be delayed—some therapists' meeting or something. They'll be half an hour late—they say. Knowing Mr. Pitz, I'd say more likely an hour. He can't bear to offend even the clock."

"Oh, well," said Miss Johnson. "I haven't any important engagements to meet, have you, Allegra? I'll just take a run down to the kitchen and see my favorite aide—Pris—she is the nicest girl." She trundled herself down the hall.

Alice felt a touch of envy of the "favorite" Pris, but still

57

she was glad of this excuse to sit down beside Mrs. Daniels.

"I'm so glad to have a chance to talk with you, child," said Mrs. Daniels. Alice felt a throb of pleasure. They both felt the same! "How's it going, anyway?"

Now the familiar sinking in Alice's stomach.

Why had she sat down?

As long as she was only expected to say the usual things, she was all right. She could pretend she was like everyone else. But to answer questions! Even "Where do you live?" confused her. Did she still, in some manner, live with her family? Anywhere else—school, Home, nursing home—was just a stopover. She didn't really live anywhere.

But "How's it going?" was even worse.

Alice smiled vaguely and started to get up so she could get away from this. But Mrs. Daniels reached out her gnarled hand and put enough pressure on Alice's thigh so that it was necessary for her to sit down again.

"Yes, isn't it funny how the easiest questions are impossible to answer?" Mrs. Daniels said. "They're always asking me, 'How are you?' What am I to say? 'I had a stroke, but I got over it, so I'm fine, but I can't do a thing'? 'My loving daughter-in-law sent me to this place so I would get much better care than she and my son could give me. Isn't that great?' But I feel rotten."

Alice gripped her hands together. What should she say now? Nobody ever talked to her about how they felt.

"Do *you* feel rotten?" asked Mrs. Daniels.

. . . But you didn't *say* that!

"Most people do, most of the time, you know," said Mrs. Daniels cheerfully. "Now, take Ginger Man. You know who I mean? That boy who helps with the therapy?"

58

Alice nodded. She could remember him clearly, his broad shoulders and freckled face. His hair was red.

"That's why you call him Ginger Man," she said suddenly.

"Whoa! . . . Oh, you mean his hair. Well, that's not the only reason. There's more—quite a lot more. Did you realize he's deaf and dumb?"

"Oh!"

Of all the strange people Alice had met, she had never before met a deaf and dumb person.

"Yes, it is surprising, isn't it? You'd think, until you knew him, that it would make him different. Well, he is different, but not as you would expect. He reads lips, of course, but I tell him he can read my mind, too. He knows exactly what to do and when to do it. But he can't speak at all. Somebody brought him up with lip-reading and sign language only. He writes, too, very well. But I tell him he has a third mode—that is to say, a third voice. With some people there's only one, yak, yak, yak. Others can put themselves across in writing. But he, Ginger Man, uses touch. That's a way of communicating, too."

Alice said suddenly, "I'm glad." She didn't know quite why.

Mrs. Daniels did. "I know. I feel the same way. It makes us all greater, to know someone who overcomes a handicap, like that—who finds another way. Because we all have them—handicaps, I mean."

Alice sneaked a glance at Mrs. Daniels to see if she was trying to make a point. People always said this. Over and over again, looking from platforms, down on her and all the other children who had been herded into rows of seats on purpose to hear it, and whose heads bobbed, not because they agreed, but because they were sleepy. (And some of them, too, because their necks were weak.)

Alice hoped Mrs. Daniels would realize she had said something dumb and take it back. But this time she didn't seem to know, as she had before, what Alice's stillness meant. She was looking off into the distance.

"My youngest son was one. He was beautiful, gifted, kind, sensitive . . . Yet he couldn't make it. And finally, he killed himself."

Alice was shocked horribly. "Did you put him in a home?"

Mrs. Daniels suddenly noticed her again. "Why—why, yes, finally we did. After everything else had failed."

They seemed to sit there silently for a long time. They were roused by a loud eerie cry from the public address system.

"Alice!" it croaked, unbelievably. "Alice! Calling the aide, Alice! Where is Miss Johnson? Where is Miss Johnson?"

Alice jumped up and ran down the corridor where Miss Johnson had disappeared. The corridor turned a corner. At the end of it was an open door, through which Alice could see the bushes, misted with green, and the empty drive.

5

ALICE rushed down the drive and looked both ways along the sidewalk. Nothing. Nobody. And where was the hospital? "Down the street," Miss Johnson had said. But Alice could see only another house and the slope to the river. Well, it must be down some other street.

Feeling that she shouldn't waste a minute, Alice chose a direction at random and sped along. Still nothing. Then another corner. Surely she shouldn't go downhill to the river, so she turned the opposite way and ran another block. Still, no hospital.

She began to realize she should have simply told someone in the nursing home where she thought Miss Johnson had gone. *They* would know where the hospital was. Well, so would anybody who lived around here. She'd better go to a house and ask. Though that was very hard.

While she was hesitating, somebody backed a car out of a drive. Alice ran, waving frantically, to intercept them, but the driver was craning over his shoulder as he backed, and didn't see her. She went up the walk and rang the doorbell. No answer. Of course! The person in that house had just driven away. She felt too discouraged to try another house.

She decided to go back to the nursing home. She was wasting too much time, and who knew what might happen to poor Miss Johnson, ninety-eight years old, out alone in her wheelchair. Alice started running again at the thought, but soon slowed in despair. There was no use running when she didn't know where she was running to.

She didn't even know how to get back to the nursing home. She looked in all directions, hoping to locate at least the river. Oh! There was something—some high roofs peeking over a weedy hill. That must be the hospital.

Down another block, and the view opened out before her, just beyond a hill that was, in truth, as she remembered now, across the street from the nursing home.

And there, crossing the street with the green light, was the wheelchair! It was moving very slowly, irregularly, jerking along, starting up and then almost stopping. And now the light changed, and there were several cars threatening the crossing.

Alice disregarded them and charged across. Miss Johnson looked over her shoulder.

"Oh, dear, so you caught me," she said, and gave a little sobbing laugh. "Well, as a matter of fact, dear, I'm rather glad. I'm too exhausted to go much further, and I surely wouldn't do my poor niece much good if they brought me in dead."

Alice didn't say anything, just turned the wheelchair around, and when the light had changed, started pushing it back as fast as she could over the uneven walk.

Miss Johnson slept all the way, even over curbs.

When they were about half a block from the nursing

home, Mr. Bell's long black car pulled up alongside, and Mr. Bell yelled out the window, "Is she all right?"

Miss Johnson woke up and gave a feeble wave. "Mercy, yes. Of course I am," she whispered, so faintly that even Alice could hardly hear her.

Almost the whole nursing home staff was drawn up at the entrance when Alice wheeled her patient up the drive.

"I've rarely made a more dramatic entrance," whispered Miss Johnson. She giggled. But Alice knew it wasn't funny. The aides stared at her solemnly, the nurses ignored her, and everyone rushed out to swarm around Miss Johnson and took the wheelchair out of Alice's hands.

Mr. Bell, having parked, spoke to Alice in passing, on his way to join the crowd. "Come to my office immediately before lunch," he said. "There'll be a meeting of all staff."

On account of her, no doubt. They would scold her. How she hated to be scolded.

But it wasn't lunchtime yet. Alice went up to second floor to help with the lunch trays for the patients.

The nurse at the desk never lifted her head. The lunches came up on the elevator, and Brownie rolled the carts out; Pan went along to distribute the trays.

"Shall I help you?" asked Alice. Pan looked at her as if she didn't recognize her and said, "If you want." It was as if suddenly Alice had almost ceased to exist.

Everybody knew. She was in disgrace. As usual, Alice felt as if it was probably true she'd done wrong, but she tried in her mind feebly to argue back.

She had only let Miss Johnson go down the hall to see that nice aide, Pris. What was wrong with that?

Plenty. For Miss Johnson had given her the slip. You should never trust the patients.

She was in no hurry to get to Mr. Bell's office.

She went up to her room, combed her hair, looked at a spot on her forehead, then realized she would be late—as bad as being early. Sure enough, she was about the last one there. The chairs were all full. They seemed to be waiting for her. Mr. Bell said, "Alice, come up here please."

There was an empty chair on Mr. Bell's side of the desk, facing everybody. Alice sat in it and looked at her hands. Would they punish her? Call the police? Send her to jail? This must be the worst thing she had ever done. She'd never been set up in front of everybody, like this, for her disgrace.

Why had she ever come to this nursing home? She should have kicked and screamed. She should have gone home when her father asked her. She should have never let them take her out of the safety of some place made for people like her. That was the trouble, and that was their fault, they should have known. It was Mrs. Hones's fault. Everybody was against her, even her mother had finally turned against her, "This is too much," her mother had said. Why, she thought in terror, she was even against herself. Everything she did always turned out wrong.

Mr. Bell banged the desk. The quiet when she came in had filled up again with whispers, even half-smothered laughter. "Quiet, everybody!"

All right, she would not do anything, ever again. She would just sit there with her eyes down and not even be there. They couldn't get to her, then; or at least, they wouldn't know whether or not she heard or understood. She would pretend not to, even if she did.

"I have called you here today to consider a very serious matter. While it only directly concerns one person, it does concern us all indirectly. I think it would be very educational for us to take the matter up publicly, for I'm sure many of you have been just as guilty of neglecting your patients as this person I speak of today, but have just been lucky enough not to have anything serious happen as a result. We must all be more careful. We've all got to watch our step."

He moved the paperweight to the right and the bowl of daffodils (artificial—Alice had felt them one day) to the left.

"I've been planning to bring a matter to your attention, and this is the perfect opportunity. The fact is, I've been noticing for some time a certain carelessness on the part of most of you. The problem comes at the point of turnover, where one of you leaves his patient, say in therapy, and expects somebody else to take over. This is OK, if the other person is really on the job. But what if he's not? You can't count on anybody but yourself. As you know, this was the problem today; the person involved shrugged off her responsibility before anyone else took over."

Mr. Bell moved the paperweight to the left, and the bowl of flowers to the right.

"A small lapse, you might say, but it could have been fatal. A ninety-eight-year-old woman was at stake! It was a lapse of judgment, nothing more; no bad intention, no bad temper. But it is terribly serious. For the sake of the institution, and the morale of all of you, I'm sorry to say I shall have to let this person go."

"I guess that's all. Unless anybody has anything to add."

There was a ringing silence. It was all over for Alice. What could anyone say?

Then suddenly somebody did say something. It was Appolonia. The words came from behind Alice, but there was no mistaking that sharp, positive voice.

"What the heck! If we're all careless, then why take it out on Alice? Besides, I don't think it was her fault."

Mr. Bell's hands stopped lighting his cigarette.

"Appolonia, I'd advise you to slow down," he said. His voice, very calm and low while he delivered the sentence on Alice, had risen several notes. "You're popping off again, and if you remember, we agreed last time—"

"Oh, come on, I'm not popping off, as you call it. If you don't know that, you're dumber than I think you are."

Appolonia was now standing in front of the desk, her arms folded across her chest, and it seemed to Alice she must be six feet tall. She was so thin, and so dark, and so straight! And her face with its high curved nose and flashing eyes under the cloud of hair was blazing.

"Sure Miss Johnson ran away; and do you know why? Well, I do. First off, she got loose because somebody made a mistake and didn't tell the floors the therapists would be late. Second, she got loose because somebody who shoulda been on duty in the kitchen was out of line. But in the third place, and it should be first place, really, she got loose because nobody in this whole God-damned place ever had sense enough to figure out what she wanted! Nobody but one. The one person who listened to Miss Johnson and knew she just wanted to get out so's she could visit her niece in the hospital—the one person who cared about how she felt—is the same person you're kicking out!"

66

What *was* going on? Appolonia—defending her?

"Yeah—and if Alice hadn't listened—if she'd turned off like all the rest of us—'yes honey, no honey'—what woulda happened then? Nobody else knew where Miss Johnson went."

"Oh, come on, Appo, don't make a Federal case of it," said Mr. Bell. He got up from his desk, his cigarette still unlit between his fingers. "I've made my decision. Let's adjourn."

But Appolonia still stood there, and everybody else was silent, waiting, alert for more excitement.

"Yeah!" Appolonia said tauntingly. "What if the old lady'd got to the hospital, which she was just about to do, if Alice hadn't come. What do you s'pose she woulda told 'em?"

She let that hang in the air, but when Mr. Bell opened his mouth, she cut in: "It would have all come out! Can't you see the headlines! 'Ninety-Eight-Year-Old Nursing Home Patient Escapes to Hospital!' Everybody would say, 'What nursing home was that?' Then they'd say, 'Oh! Well, I'd never send my mother to that place.'"

"OK, OK, everybody's dismissed," said Mr. Bell. "All but Appolonia." He finally lighted his cigarette.

"Why don't you sit down and try to get calm, Appolonia," he said, after a puff or two. "What a temper you've got! But there is something in what you say. It wasn't just Alice— there were others involved. But when you think what might have happened—"

"It did happen," said Appolonia. She was still standing.

"Well, I mean if the old lady had been injured or something—"

"She was injured, by nobody paying attention to what she needed."

"Come on," said Mr. Bell harshly. "Stop harping! Well, Alice, have you learned your lesson? Maybe we should give you another chance!"

He beamed, as if he were giving her a present.

"I don't know," said Alice without any expression at all. It was true: she didn't.

"Oh, I guess we might let it pass this time. Careful does it, right? I expect your father will be in later—I called him up to tell him what happened, and that I was afraid you weren't going to work out. So I expect you can tell him I've given you another chance, OK? Well, you girls better get down to lunch before the food's all gone, right?"

Appolonia beckoned Alice with a nod. As they went out the door, she actually put her arm around Alice's shoulders.

"We killed him," she murmured, with a ripple in her voice. "We slaughtered the old bastard. But we better watch our step from now on—he never forgets, and he'll be waiting to get back at us, for sure!"

6

ALICE chewed and looked at her plate during lunch, concentrating on not finding out if people were looking at her.

She could hardly wait to get to the privacy of her room; but there, sitting on her bed as if she owned it, was Mrs. Hones.

Mrs. Hones jumped up and ran over to Alice, almost as if she intended to put her arms around her. But Alice stood so stiff and still that Mrs. Hones's arms fell down at her sides.

"Did you ever hear of such a thing—they didn't even call me!" she cried. "Leaming finally had sense enough to let me know, but Bell would have fired you without even consulting me! Maybe I'm just a welfare investigator, not a real social worker, but by golly, I do have some interest in my clients!"

"Oh, well," said Alice. She still wasn't sure she wanted Mrs. Hones to have an interest in her.

"Well, you are calm," said Mrs. Hones, looking at her curiously. "What do you think about Appolonia now?"

Alice shrugged. She hadn't figured it out yet.

"Ye gods, don't you realize what she did for you?"

"Appolonia doesn't like Mr. Bell."

Mrs. Hones lifted her hands in the air. Then she laughed. "OK, OK, I give up. Out of the mouths of babes . . . Well, anyway, I'm glad it came out all right. You did show up pretty good, knowing what was going on in that old lady's mind. By the way, you got your first paycheck, Mrs. Leaming says. You'd better let me take care of it. I'll leave you some for spending money and bank the rest for you."

Alice looked back at Mrs. Hones in her dullest manner, her eyes half-closed. The money was under the lining paper in her dresser drawer, and she wasn't going to let Mrs. Hones take care of a penny.

"Oh! All right," said Mrs. Hones, and she whistled between her teeth. "If that's the way you feel about it, I'll just get them to hold the check till I come, next time."

"You can't do that unless I say so, it's against the law," said Alice. The girls at the home had told her that. It was one of their favorite topics.

"You don't think I intend to steal your money?" cried Mrs. Hones. She was really mad, now. "I just want to keep it safe, so you'll have something to show for your hard work. Any time you want to spend some of it on something reasonable, you have only to tell me."

"I can take care of it," said Alice. "I like money."

She hadn't considered it before, but now she realized that, though at first she had only thought about things she could buy, now she got a kick out of just having that money. She was going to keep it safe.

Mrs. Hones let out her madness in a gruff little laugh. "You're something else, you know that? But how do you know you can keep your money safe? There's a problem of stealing here, you know. Nobody can hang on to anything valuable, unless it's in the safe."

"Then I'll put it in the safe," said Alice, pleased with this idea, as she had worried about her hiding place. She was not afraid of Francine's taking it, but she had an idea that Billy Lass Holder, in the room next door, might take a notion to do a little exploring.

"You beat me," said Mrs. Hones, laughing again, this time more easily. "OK, seems you need me about as much as you need a hole in your head—especially with Appolonia on your side. Better keep her that way."

And she left.

Alice combed her hair. She felt rather good. She combed her hair a lot now, and it looked better. But there were still spots on her complexion, and she wondered if that nurse at the home was right when she said it would help to eat more fruit and vegetables. She might try it. She might even get really pretty.

When she was a little girl, she had thought she was pretty (Mama had told her that once), and she used to go around asking people, "I'm pretty, don't you think? Don't you think I'm pretty?"

But though some people said yes, they always looked away from her eyes when they said it, so she decided she must be wrong. Of course, people usually looked away from her eyes when she said anything; that was why she'd almost quit talking.

Now it was time for her to go back to the floor and get the patients down for their naps. She covered one side of the corridor, but as she started back up the other side, the nurse at the desk beckoned.

"They want you to report to the office, Alice."

Alice looked at her in alarm.

"You have visitors."

Visitors! How could she have visitors? She had nobody to visit her.

Then she remembered what Mr. Bell had said: "I called your father." Oh, dear. She felt terribly guilty, visualizing Dad's worried face. Dad was always worried about her. Mama used to not be. But then she changed.

The parlor where patients entertained their visitors was just across from the main office. There was the beauty parlor, and there was the activities room, and off to the left was the parlor. Maria took charge of all these places and had already asked Alice if she didn't want to sneak in on her afternoon off and have a permanent.

"Hi, there, Beautiful!" she called now, looking up over the bowed shoulders and absorbed face of an old woman who was weaving something on a loom. "When you coming in to let me fix you all up?"

Alice said, "Pretty soon." She didn't believe in all that "beautiful" stuff, because she knew Maria called everybody that, even the ugliest old woman in the place, old Miss Scampi, who had cancer of the nose.

Then she came to the parlor, and oh-oh! not only Dad, but Carol too.

They just sat and watched her as she came in. Dad looked grayer and more tired than ever. Even his tie was gray. Mama used to wear pretty things. Carol dressed fancy, too.

They waited for her to sit down near them. It was as if they were looking at her through a glass wall. Or as if she were the polar bear on the other side of the moat.

72

Then Dad said, "What are they doing to you, Baby? First they call and say you did something wrong, and just now they stop me as we come in and say you didn't do it after all."

Alice tried to think of some way to explain, but couldn't. "It was just an accident," she said.

"No, no, now really," said Carol. "Try to tell us. They said first you let somebody get away, didn't watch her right, or something. And now they say it's all right, you brought her back. That guy, Mr. Bell, he's nuts or something."

"Try to think, Baby," said Dad. "Try to tell us from the beginning."

It confused her, Dad's calling her "Baby" like that. It had been Mama's name for her.

But she tried. "I did let her get away," she said slowly. "But I didn't know she was going. But I did know where she would go, so I went after her and brought her back."

Dad and Carol glanced at each other, and then back at her.

"Well, doggone if that isn't pretty clear and straight," said Dad. "How come *you* knew, when, they say, nobody else did?"

How to tell them? Just then Appolonia came hurrying down the hall. Oh, good, thought Alice. I'll call her, and she'll explain. But just as she started to call, lifting her hand even, and just as Appolonia, noticing, paused, another thought came to Alice, or a feeling rather, that strangled the first impulse.

So you're making friends with niggers now! Carol would say.

And Dad would look worried, as if he knew nothing good

73

could ever come from Alice. If she tried something, it failed; if she didn't try, she was lazy; if she made friends (she had, a few times, but it never turned out), they were a bad lot.

So Alice's hand dropped and she looked away from Appolonia, who, after staring for a moment from one to another of them, hurried on.

"I tell you, Alice, you don't have to put up with any guff," said Dad earnestly. He leaned forward and became very emphatic. "I know something about institutions; they're terrible. That place they sent you to when you was little—that Willow place—that was awful; and the hospital where your mother went wasn't much better. I won't stand for any more of that. You come right home now. Just say the word, and Carol and I will take you home today."

Alice was astonished. She looked at Carol, who confirmed it with a nod. "Honest, Kid, we don't want you to be unhappy. For instance, if you want to keep on working here, since this little problem whatever it was, seems to have blown over, why you could come home nights, anyway."

"That way," said Dad, "you could pay the board money to us, rather than have them take it out of your pay."

Oh.

The silence got long. "I mean, after all," said Dad, "it would help us out, too. Carol lost her job the other day . . ."

The money. It was the money. Alice didn't say a word. She thought of the polar bear, standing there and looking over the moat, and the wall, swaying back and forth. It couldn't get away. It never made a sound.

"Dad, I told you not to mention that, oh you goof!" cried Carol. She was working up a tantrum, Alice thought with interest. Since she, Alice, wasn't the object of it, she didn't mind too much. Carol could really use language; Alice had learned a lot from her.

But this time, Carol pulled herself back. Maria was leaning on the table on her elbows, watching. Carol got up and pretended to be unconcerned. "Oh, well," she said. "I guess you're OK here. I'll get another job soon. So I guess we better just let things ride on as they are, right?"

Dad hung back to shake Alice's hand. He looked as if he wanted to say something else, but he didn't.

Alice watched them out the door, Carol tripping along upright and trim in her bright yellow pants suit. Dad following like a frail bent shadow.

Other people always seemed to feel better after their families visited, which was strange, because she always felt worse.

Appolonia came by on her return trip down the hall. She stopped and faced Alice with her hands on her hips.

"You crumb," she said deliberately. "Didn't want to introduce me to your folks, did you? Afraid they'd look down on you if you acted like you even knew me!"

Alice looked past Appolonia, pretending not to see or hear her. She didn't have to tell Appolonia how she was feeling. Appolonia thought she knew it all, anyway.

"You poor little dumb crumb." Appolonia snorted, and marched on.

SOON AFTER the adventure with Miss Johnson, Alice noticed that things were getting back to normal. In other words, nobody liked her. Everyone just ignored her.

Usually when Alice changed from one place to another, she had a litle spell of hopefulness. At that foster home, for instance, after they rescued her from Willowstream, the father, especially, seemed to like her, and the mother too, some; and even the girl her own age didn't mind her. But then Alice used to stay too long in the bathroom and in the living room after dinner when they wanted to be alone. By the time Alice realized this, she was mad at them for it and stayed long on purpose; and they let her go.

And at the home, she'd been Miss Joslin's favorite until the girls got mad about it and turned on her. Miss Joslin was transferred, to everybody's sorrow, and Mike came. And Alice was the "troublemaker" who caused it.

It seemed as if she was bound to make a mistake sooner or later. And when people got mad at her about one mistake, she seemed twice as likely to make another.

So, she'd done it again; she didn't know how. Especially,

she'd done it with Appolonia, who stuck her nose in the air whenever she saw Alice and sailed past without speaking.

And the others seemed always to be laughing just before she came along or just after she left. The nurses always double-checked on everything she did, expecting it to be wrong.

"Why didn't Mr. Beidenheim finish his dinner?"

"He didn't want it." He was back from the hospital, but weaker and further away than ever; he had no appetite at all.

"That doesn't make any difference. You've got to get it down him."

But Mr. Beidenheim didn't want it down him. He wanted to tell her about his youth in Germany. So she sat with the spoon in her hand and smiled and nodded.

He told her about his wife a lot. "She was just fifteen!" Mr. Beidenheim sketched a vague shape with his trembling hands. "So *hold und schoen und rein!* The very birds in the forest sang songs to her!"

He stopped to dream of those times, and Alice seized the opportunity to try to stick the spoon in his mouth, but he put her hand aside. Was she supposed to choke him with the spoon? He smiled and fell asleep.

Alice got into terrible trouble by bringing Mr. Burket a paper bag that his friend had left at the door. It contained a bottle.

"Don't you realize you must never give a patient anything to eat or drink without the permission of the doctor?"

"I didn't know what was in the bag."

Mr. Burket, who could scarcely pull a breath into his

77

tattered lungs, had needed cheering up so badly. His eyes were worse, and he'd almost given up reading the *Times*. And the bottle had cheered him, until they took it away.

But if the nurses had mistrusted her from the start, the patients at first had liked her. They had made a lot of her when she came to take them to the sun parlor. "My darlink! My darlink! Come here already and give me my morning kiss!" Mr. Gutentag was fast to his chair, so she wasn't afraid of him and let him brush her cheek with his flabby old lips, but Nurse Boston, passing, muttered, "Disgusting!"

And Pan looked the same, when Mrs. Perciballi cried with joy at the sight of Alice, sang little songs to her in Italian, and kissed her hand whenever she could get hold of it.

Suzy would stop Alice in the hall to tell stories. Suzy could tell a story in three words. "And do, and do, and do. Oh boy!" But she uttered them in so many tones and with such a lot of feeling, that Alice found it quite interesting— like TV with the sound shut off. You could imagine anything you wanted. So Alice spent time with Suzy every day, though Pan said, "Hurry up, will you!"

But then the new aide came. Her name was Ray, and she was fat and black. Alice expected no competition at all from her. Most of the patients were white, and they complained a lot about the colored help. (Except about Appolonia and Jacques, of course, who were so special.)

Alice was told to show Ray the ropes and took this task up willingly.

"Here's the linen closet, and here's the slide to the laundry," she said, walking briskly and feeling competent.

"I can see that myself," said Ray, chewing gum with her

mouth open. "Don't bother about me, kid, I can take care of myself. I'd rather nose things out on my own." And she took off, leaving Alice to stare after her disappointedly.

By the second day, Ray knew the name of everybody on the floor, patients, nurses and aides alike; and the orderlies, black and white, had tuned up their flirting to a new high. Ray flirted right back.

Ray flirted with the patients, too—with the men. And the women, she treated like babies. She began immediately to call them by their first names.

"Come on, now, Teresa, you don't need to sing me a song," she said to Mrs. Perciballi. "I'll sing you a song. Or better yet, we'll all sing together."

She gathered the sun parlor regulars in the corner and started them singing "Old MacDonald Had a Farm." Or at least, *she* sang it, with motions, and they all stared, fascinated.

She found an old ring-toss game in a closet, and set it up in the midst of them. Even the frail Mrs. Adams joined in, and chuckled happily when she made a score. But when the clock said it was time for them to go back to their rooms, Ray got everybody in line and rolled them away without paying any attention to their complaints.

"You see, Alice," said Nurse Boston. "Ray is kind to them, but doesn't let them put it over on her."

Alice veiled her eyes and hurried to get Miss Johnson for therapy. She didn't want Ray rushing Miss Johnson down without giving her time to wash her hands; she didn't want Ray calling Miss Johnson "Annie."

"Thank goodness, it's you!" said Miss Johnson. "Isn't it the loveliest morning! The flowers will soon be blooming.

79

Why don't we get off at First Floor and just pop outdoors and look around a bit!"

"Miss Johnson, don't you remember what happened?"

"Yes, but I thought maybe I could put it over on you and really get there, this time!" said Miss Johnson cheerfully.

So that was why she was glad it was Alice. Because Alice was stupid.

The elevator door opened, and they were facing the lively therapy room. Mrs. Daniels was sitting there waiting, as she had been that other day.

"Hello, Goldenhead, how's it going?"

Alice knew Mrs. Daniels must know how things were going. Everybody had heard. And Alice did a dumb thing: she noticed how she was feeling. It had scary results, the tears welled up in her eyes.

"Take care of your patient, and then come back," said Mrs. Daniels—just in time; Miss Johnson was quietly rolling toward the exit corridor.

Alice rushed after her and stood on guard till Mr. Pitz had finished settling Mr. Gutentag, who was saying over and over again, "You're killing me! You're killing me!"

Then he turned to Miss Johnson. "Well, here we are! Here's my best girl again! Come on in and let's have an adventure! Can't have you running off with other people." Mr. Pitz teased Miss Johnson about running away, instead of pretending it hadn't happened, as most people did.

"You weren't here, that's why I did it," said Miss Johnson cockily.

"Alas, 'tis true," said Mr. Pitz as he led her tenderly up the exercise steps.

80

Alice turned back to Mrs. Daniels. Alice was in control again, and no more tears starting, but the first two were still rolling down her cheeks.

Mrs. Daniels was looking at her sternly. "You hurt Appo's feelings dreadfully. And after she had stood up for you like that."

Alice opened and shut her mouth. She had been thinking all the time about how bad everyone was being to her, and she had to grope backward for the memory of her snub to Appolonia.

"She called me a dumb crumb," said Alice, and another pair of tears came up.

"Appolonia always calls names. She fights back at the drop of a hat. She's had to," said Mrs. Daniels.

"But why me?" asked Alice, wiping the last two tears away, while others took their place.

"Because you scorned her, of course!" cried Mrs. Daniels. "You acted as if she weren't good enough to be introduced to your family!"

"It was just because she's Colored," said Alice. Why couldn't they understand?

Mrs. Daniels stared at Alice, shaking her head as she did so. "You and I are going to have to have a lot of good talks," she said. "About equality and a lot of other things. We'll get together soon. We'll arrange it on Thursday."

Alice saw that Ginger Man had appeared, and he moved up to put his hands gently on Mrs. Daniels's shoulders. But he was looking at Alice. As soon as she looked into his face, he shifted his gaze.

She continued to look at him curiously. He looked like anybody, even though he was deaf and dumb.

81

Things went on as usual for several days after that. Alice did steal a few curious looks at Appolonia to see if she could discover anything to support Mrs. Daniels's statement that Alice had hurt her feelings. But Appolonia never glanced her way and was always either talking loudly or laughing with Petrie Flynn, with whom she had lately been acting up terribly.

Ray was still the favorite of the patients, and Alice was still the laughingstock of the staff. She tried to be as unnoticeable as possible, and longed for Thursday, when she would see Mrs. Daniels again.

When she went on Thursday to wheel Miss Johnson down, she found Ray already there. "I'm taking her," said Alice.

"Not this time, you aren't. Can't you see I've got it under control?" retorted Ray, shoving Alice out of the way with her brawny shoulder. "And as you should remember, you don't!"

"Please! Please!" said Miss Johnson faintly. "I told you it's all right. I won't try anything."

"You told me!" Ray said sarcastically.

"I'm taking her!" said Alice, and she let her eyes flash. She didn't do that often. Carol had told her years ago, "You really look crazy when you do that!" And she didn't usually want to look crazy. But it worked, for Ray suddenly let go the wheelchair.

"Oh, well, OK, if you feel that bad about it," she said, and bustled away.

Miss Johnson said nothing as Alice rolled her down the hall. Which was unusual. She must be depressed.

"Didn't they ever take you to the hospital to see your

niece yet?" Alice asked, though she knew it was wrong to ask. The aides were not supposed to get into the patients' private business, and certainly never to criticize the staff to them.

"You would think they would, wouldn't you?" Miss Johnson asked fiercely.

This almost drove the thought of Mrs. Daniels out of Alice's mind, but when the elevator doors opened, she remembered, and her eyes flew to Mrs. Daniels's regular spot. Nobody there!

Alice delivered Miss Johnson to Mr. Pitz, but her whole insides felt sick and empty. Mrs. Daniels had said, "See you on Thursday," and now she wasn't here. Maybe she was mad at Alice, too.

As she went back to the elevator, she noticed that her shoulders were bent, just like her father's.

Someone touched her gently on the back.

Turning around, she saw Ginger Man standing there. This time he was looking steadily at her. He held up a piece of paper. On it something was printed, and printed very clearly; Alice thought how well it was printed, and then realized he meant her to read it. He was waiting for her to do so.

SHE HAD A STROKE

Alice read it and didn't understand, looked into Ginger Man's face again. He was nodding sadly. She wanted to cry, though she didn't quite get it. Why, Mrs. Daniels was all right only Monday! He answered her bewildered look by writing some more.

MRS. DANIELS GOT SICK. SHE IS IN THE HOSPITAL.

Oh! Oh! This was the way things always happened! Alice

thought she would never get used to it. Mama had said, "I can't stand it any more," and sent Alice away and went to the hospital and died. And now Mrs. Daniels, who called her Goldenhead, now she was sick and soon she would die.

Alice caught her lower lip between her teeth and stared at Ginger Man without seeing him. He took the paper back and wrote again.

SHE WILL GET WELL

Alice looked straight in his face to see if he really meant it, if it was true. Yes! At least, he thought it was true! He kept nodding, and he smiled. It must be true!

Alice was so relieved that she felt like laughing. She did laugh.

Ginger Man's joy also got too much for just a smile. He reached out and touched Alice's cheek.

The touch drove through Alice like a red-hot poker.

"Never let a man touch you," they had told her—everyone had told her. "They will take advantage of you every time."

Alice jerked away, and their smiles faded at the same moment.

Alice turned her back on the surprise and shock in Ginger Man's face.

8

THERE WAS a commotion on second floor one morning.

Oh-oh! Alice thought. For a commotion always meant some bad thing. It might be a death or a broken hip or maybe only a tantrum. There was never any excitement over something good.

But then—what good ever happened in a nursing home?

Well, Mr. Burket's nephew from San Francisco had come to visit last week. That was good. Mr. Burket's face had been dark red with happiness, and the nephew brought a bottle, and he and Alice hid it.

But this commotion was a tantrum. Mrs. Witherspoon was having it.

"I won't! I won't! I won't go into that room down the hall. It doesn't have a private bath, and I arranged for a private bath!" Mrs. Witherspoon was hollering. Pan and Appolonia were trying to lift her out of bed into the wheelchair, and she was hanging on to the mattress for dear life.

"I can't manage it. We'll never get out this way. Hey, Alice, run and get an orderly," gasped Pan. She herself was good and hefty, but Mrs. Witherspoon was at least two hundred pounds of dead—or fighting—weight.

"Right," said Alice. "But why are they moving her?"

She didn't usually ask for whys and wherefores, but this time she suspected—she hoped—

"Leg's coming back from the hospital," said Pan. "We've got to have her on Second, and near the nurse's station, and with a private bath. She's in bad shape."

Alice ran as fast as she could down the hall. "In bad shape," but at least she was coming back.

Petrie was dressing Mr. Burket's foot. He was good at dressing wounds, and they let him do it even if he was only an orderly, because he was going to medical school.

"Appo says come quick," said Alice. Appo hadn't said a darn thing about speed, but Alice thought Petrie would be quicker to go if he thought she had. "They're having a time with Mrs. Witherspoon."

"That old fool," said Petrie, laying Mr. Burket's foot carefully on the footstool.

The elevator door opened, and a stretcher was rolled out. Already! Alice craned to see over the covers and wrappings. That rough white head! Oh, good!

She followed the stretcher down the hall. At the desk, she heard Nurse Boston on the phone. ". . . but she's really in a state, Mr. Witherspoon. I do wish you'd come over here and see if you can calm her down."

Alice had to distribute lunches, so she only picked up odds and ends of what was happening. Mrs. Witherspoon had been wheeled down the hall and wasn't yelling any more. What had Petrie done to quiet her? Mrs. Daniels was lying like a log in the bed in Mrs. Witherspoon's old room, with Mrs. Symes peering eagerly over at her.

As soon as you had taken around all the trays, you had

to go back and pick them up. Alice stopped to try to help Mr. Beidenheim eat a little before she took his tray away. Down at the end of the corridor, where Mrs. Witherspoon's new room was, she paused curiously to find out how things were going.

A large middle-aged man in a heavy overcoat was in there. "You be quiet, Mother," he was saying, his voice as hard as iron. "If they throw you out of this nursing home, it's about curtains for you. There's not another one in the county that will take you, and we'll just have to send you back to that dump in the Bronx that you hate. You just have to make up your mind to try to act decent for a change."

Mrs. Witherspoon was quiet at last. Alice could hardly believe it was really she, looking up at her son with mournful eyes, hands clutched together on her chest, without a word to say.

That son was really talking mean.

He took his fine overcoat down in the elevator, and then —my goodness! A new commotion arose. Petrie and Appolonia fighting!

"You big black son-of-a-gun, I didn't tell you to hurt her!" Appolonia was screaming, beating at Petrie with her fists. He was not really fighting back, only trying to protect himself. It was funny to see Petrie, that great strong man, huddled behind his arms as Appo hailed down blows upon him.

"Hey, cut it out! I didn't hurt her. To speak of. I had to get a hold on her so she wouldn't scratch my eyes out. You sent for me to move her."

"Well, I didn't, but that's beside the point. Aren't you the guy who wants to be a doctor? What for? The money?"

87

Petrie grabbed Appo's wrists and looked at her fiercely. "For money and other stuff. What's the matter with money? And whoever had any reason to be nice to Mrs. Witherspoon?"

"You're letting it get to you around here," said Appolonia. To Alice's amazement, she was sobbing as she struggled to get free from Petrie and rushed down the hall.

Petrie looked after her. "What a dog!" he muttered. His eyes fell on Alice. "Ain't she something? What do you think of her, you sweet little blonde nothing? Exact opposites, ain't you? Come to think of it, you got a distinct advantage."

"Well," said Alice. She was surprised, but her words kept coming. "Well," she said, "that old lady's got a mean good-for-nothing son. She's helpless, that's why she yells. She doesn't need you to hurt her, too."

Petrie stared.

Alice said smartly, "Close your mouth."

Petrie gave a huge laugh. "Well, I'll be damned. You sweet little blonde nothing! You *aren't* opposites!"

Alice didn't know what he meant.

She went back to see if Mrs. Daniels was awake yet.

At least Mrs. Daniels was not asleep. Her eyes were wide open. Alice moved hesitantly into their range. When she was sure they were looking directly at her, she started to smile. She tried to smile. But nothing happened in return. The sunken lips didn't move; the staring eyes didn't waver. Alice's smile quivered away, and after a moment of solemn staring, she backed out.

In the corridor they were still talking about the Witherspoon excitement.

"If it weren't so maddening, it would be funny," said Pan. "I hear she's been on relief for years. 'Reserved a private room!' Maybe she did in the first place . . ."

"For three months, till her savings ran out," said Nurse Boston.

"Shall we tell Mr. Bell?"

"He'll throw her out. He's been dying for an excuse," said Appolonia.

"I can't stand Mrs. Witherspoon until I see her son," said Pan.

"Well, he's probably like he is because of her," said Appolonia. "Rotten parents have rotten children."

But Alice knew something else. Good parents could have worthless children. Daddy might not be so hot, but he was all right, and Mama had been—Mama. Yet look at her own daughter, Alice.

9

"ALICE! Mrs. Daniels needs the bedpan . . ."

"Alice, will you try to get Mrs. Daniels to eat her breakfast?"

It came to be accepted that Mrs. Daniels was Alice's patient, the reason being, of course, that nobody else wanted the struggle. There was no glory in it, and it was hard, and it was unpleasant, to push puréed food through the slack lips and wait while the hard old empty gums mumbled the food automatically, and the wrinkled old throat swallowed it down. Sometimes it swallowed the wrong way and choked, and then Alice would follow the procedure Nurse Boston taught her, slipping her arm under Mrs. Daniels's shoulders and holding her up while she gasped her windpipe free, often spraying food all over the bed and Alice in the process. Alice didn't like that at all.

The doctor looked in daily. He said Mrs. Daniels had had a series of small strokes, but nothing requiring more hospitalization at the moment.

"Just keep her contented," he told Nurse Boston, and Nurse Boston nodded at Alice after he had gone, and said, "Did you understand?"

Alice nodded, but thought, *contented!* She was the one who most often received the full glare of Leg's despairing old eyes. Leg's pain made Alice ache.

But Alice at least stayed. Nobody else wanted to think about Leg. Sometimes they didn't even want Alice to think about her.

"Come on, get out of there, we need you on the floor," Pan would complain, looking in to find Alice holding Mrs. Daniels's hand. Alice would jump quickly up and start changing the sheet or regulating the catheter. But she didn't fool Pan. "She doesn't know anything, so why waste all that time on tender loving care?"

Alice knew better. The stroking of the hands (bundles of brittle old sticks held together by papery skin) would quiet the eyes' desperation. Finally eyes would close, and Leg would begin to snore. Then Alice would steal away.

Mrs. Daniels's son came to visit, with his wife. They had been there before—Alice had heard the others speak of it —but she had not seen them. She scarcely saw them this time. She ran away.

She had only one glimpse of a tall man with a high-bridged nose like his mother's. In no other way did he resemble the untidy ragbag of a Leg; he was smooth and elegant. And his wife was so different from the fattish ladies in print dresses who were the daughters. (Alice generally thought of them as the mothers, because in their bulky anxiety or disapproval they were the guardians of the frail wisps they visited.)

"I do hope Mother will tolerate our gifts this time," the slender and lovely lady said anxiously.

That was when Alice hurried out of hearing.

When she came back the visitors were gone, the flowers were wilting on the dresser, and Pan and Petrie were sampling the candy.

And the old lady was staring at the ceiling, same as ever.

One day, there was a change, but it wasn't much of an improvement. At least, it didn't seem to be at first.

Alice had sat down beside the bed to do the daily hand-stroking, having finished the bedpan and bath routine. But she wasn't thinking about what she was doing, for her mind was wandering in a sort of forest of half-recognizable people.

There was Francine with her glasses pushed up on her forehead as she raised her eyes from her books and asked Alice how she was doing, barely waiting for an answer. She always studied in their room now, without worrying about Alice's slumbers, but they still hadn't had that good talk. Then there was Ray, strutting along the hall, shoving Miss Johnson's chair ahead of her. Appolonia, leaping along like a goat, and Petrie galloping after . . . while Dad and Carol and Ernie peered at the whole thing from behind the safety of the porch railing at home.

And over there by himself stood Ginger Man, gazing at her and Mrs. Daniels from a distance, patiently and sadly saying (but not in words) that it was all going to be all right, and why had Alice jumped away from him?

That was the way he always seemed when she saw him twice a week, as she took Miss Johnson to therapy. He looked at her carefully, seeming to pull the news about Mrs. Daniels from her face. It was never good, of course. And then he would give that little nod and sigh that meant OK then, better news next time, and go about his business.

92

It was strange. She never spoke to him, and yet they discussed Mrs. Daniels. He had never written any more notes for her, and certainly never touched her again, but he was the only one who paid any attention to her, now that Leg was out of it.

It was funny, the different ways people paid attention to each other. She noticed that about other people, too. Appolonia never spoke to Petrie any more, but flirted with Jacques. Why did Petrie go for walks with, of all people, Francine?

Alice was especially mystified about what went on between boys and girls.

She had been at one institution that took care of boys as well as girls, but that was the frightening Willowstream School, where all the patients were so anxious and scared that they never thought whether they themselves were girls or boys, let alone anybody else.

There had been all that talk about boys and men at the home, but it didn't seem to make sense. One day the stories would seem to mean the exact opposite of what had been said just as positively the day before. Alice had a confused idea of what "guys" were really like. They were wonderful; they were awful; they were dangerous; they could give a girl a lot of fun, but also hurt her, and make her pregnant— that was the worst thing of all.

Ginger Man didn't seem to fit any of these ideas. Like Ernie—Ernie was a guy, too, but he didn't seem like one of those terrible creatures they talked about. But not wonderful, either.

Could Jacques and Petrie and Ginger Man be sort of like

Ernie? Not all good or bad, but sort of in between—like girls?

But they were not like girls, they were different. That was why Alice had to think about them so much.

All of a sudden her thoughts were jerked back into here and now. Mrs. Daniels's hand plunged in hers. In fact, it plunged out of hers. Alice's startled eyes found Mrs. Daniels looking straight at her, and instead of being dull and suffering, her look flashed with anger.

" 'Top 'at! 'Top! 'Is minute! Immediately!"

Alice pulled her hand away, as if from a burning stove. Mrs. Daniels hadn't said a word since her last stroke, and though her speech wasn't clear, Alice could tell what she meant, all right!

"Too hard! Hurt!" Mrs. Daniels continued indignantly.

Then she closed her eyes and began to snore.

Alice watched a minute, then got up softly and hurried out. She was quite mad and hurt, halfway down the hall. Then she suddenly began to smile.

It was so like Mrs. Daniels to get mad at having her hand stroked! She wasn't a lap dog, Alice could hear her saying. Well, but when you were so sick, Alice told her silently, it made you feel better; you know it did.

She didn't know what to expect when she went in next day to give the bath. She stopped cautiously a couple of feet short of the bed.

Mrs. Daniels's eyes were wide open and turned in her direction, but without expression. Alice was disappointed, but in a way relieved, too. The sudden outburst must have been merely momentary. But as she moved with more assurance toward the bed, the strident voice broke forth again.

" 'Cared you, di'n't I?"

And Mrs. Daniels began to laugh. She laughed and laughed, and lifted her shaking hand to wipe the drool from her mouth. And Alice laughed, too. Alice seldom laughed. It felt funny to be laughing, with someone else—about what?

"Come on, 'troke me, I dare you!" Mrs. Daniels held out her purplish bundle of sticks and laughed again.

Alice bathed her, getting a few criticisms of her technique, but doing fairly well; she was so used to doing it now, having practiced up when Mrs. Daniels, so to speak, wasn't looking.

But after that, she was at a loss. It was her scheduled time to soothe. And she couldn't do that any more, obviously, but she didn't feel like rushing off without some kind of expression of what she felt—thankfulness.

" 'At fine," said Mrs. Daniels comfortably, as Alice hesitated. "No need nothing more now. T'morra I better, we talk."

Alice looked forward to this impatiently, but nervously; and next day it happened. But Mrs. Daniels surprised her (she always surprised her) by not wanting to talk about herself, but about Alice.

"Tell me 'bout your fam'ly."

Alice was paralyzed. All the parts of her past seemed to fly out in different directions.

"Mother? Father?"

"My mother died," said Alice. "Long ago." When was it? She only knew it had happened soon after she was sent away from home. Sometimes it seemed as if it had happened first.

"Brothers? Sisters?"

Alice held up one finger on each hand. It struck her that she had not used that way of answering since—long ago. She used to hold up three fingers, then four, then five. Why? —oh, yes, to show her age. Mama had taught her.

"They visit?" asked Mrs. Daniels.

Alice looked back blankly. She didn't want to say they did visit (for somehow, they didn't, really), but she couldn't exactly say no.

"Hard to visit 'body sick or—sad," said Mrs. Daniels. Alice wondered if Mrs. Daniels's family visited any oftener (or better) than Alice's. Surely they must.

Soon after that, they did visit. This time they caught Alice sitting on the bed. Mrs. Daniels had said something funny, and they were both laughing. Whatever it was they'd been laughing about, it popped out of Alice's head the moment she saw the two of them standing there so tall and handsome. Everything was solemn on the instant.

"Hello, Mother," said the son, coming to the bed and bending down for a quick touch of lips to forehead. "How are you today?"

"You really wanta know?" Mrs. Daniels asked severely. She could say her words quite well now, but she left out some, and put in "a" whenever she needed a filler.

"Of course we do, darling," said the lady, floating across the room in a cloud of wonderful perfume. "And we can tell at a glance that you're much improved."

"We'd have been here sooner, only I had to run over to London, and Joyce went with me."

"Hey! Alice with golden!" cried Mrs. Daniels, catching Alice just as she tried to slip out the door. "Come back and meet a! Here a girl that care for me well. Here my greatest son, Alice, and dau-in-law to match." She laughed quite hard.

After a scared look at each of them (they didn't laugh), Alice got away.

She was so flustered that she started down the hall in the wrong direction. When she noticed this, she turned around; repassing the open door, she heard the son say, "Why Mother, is that the retarded girl you told us about? Are you sure she's adequate? Maybe we should insist on your having someone else."

Before Alice could scurry out of range, she heard Mrs. Daniels's answer.

"You leave her 'lone. She my friend."

10

"ALICE, Leg says to get your ass down to Second as fast as you can wiggle."

Alice was already going to Second as fast as she could wiggle. Browny was leering at her, trying her out. Alice was scared, but a little pleased, too, that an orderly would speak to her at all.

"She did not," said Alice, rousing her courage to try to talk as the other girls did—snappy.

"She just the same as did, that's what she meant," said Browny. "My God, how that dame throws her weight around!"

"She does not," said Alice.

Browny screwed up his face and went whistling off down the hall, indicating to Alice by his slanting shoulder and shuffling step that she was still a creep. Alice wondered what she should have said. Perhaps she should have said, "She sure does!" And she would have said it if she had thought of it, for talking mean about the patients was always the right thing to do.

She wouldn't mind being mean to Leg off where Leg

wouldn't hear. But not to have her know. Leg might mind. She liked Alice. "She my friend." But Leg wouldn't ever have known if Alice had said, "She sure does!" to Browny; and besides, it was true: Leg did throw her weight around.

She asked Alice to do impossible things. What would it be this time? Alice went in, as always, with as much anxiety as anticipation.

Mrs. Daniels was sitting on the edge of her bed, still in her nightgown, and her short white hair hadn't even been combed. She was pawing wildly through the drawer of the night table.

"My teef! They 'tole my teef!" she cried, glancing at Alice. "You go tell 'em I know all about it, and they better bring 'em back at once. You hurry."

Alice looked at her in silent discouragement before she turned back down the hall again. This was one of those days when Leg hardly seemed to know who Alice was, let alone any golden hair nonsense.

The nurse was just as mad at Alice for delivering the message as Leg had been when she sent it.

"Well, why don't you handle it yourself? You know I don't have the faintest idea where her teeth are. Or rather, I can give a good guess, and so could you: she's thrown them away again!"

Alice squeezed her hands together in distress. She couldn't deny it. She hadn't believed it at first—that the wise and wonderful Leg could wrap her plate in toilet paper and throw it in the wastebasket and then forget all about it; but now she knew, for Petrie had found it there when he was cleaning the room, and nobody else could have done it.

But Alice simply couldn't go and tell Leg that. She couldn't. She wouldn't. She stood there with her mouth open.

The nurse examined her face and sighed. "Oh, well. I guess I'll have to do it myself."

Alice slunk after her and stood with her eyes on the floor while Nurse Boston gave it to Leg.

"Why don't you take care of your teeth? You know that you're always the one that loses them." The nurse shuffled through the wastebasket, found nothing, and rudely elbowed Leg away from the drawer. In a moment she pulled out the pink shell with its crescent of white teeth and held it up accusingly.

"Oh. There it is," said Leg calmly, seized it and shoved it in. "Thanks, Nurse."

The nurse snorted and went away.

"You may do my hair now, Alice," said Leg, holding out the brush.

Now Alice's heart rose like a bubble! She took the brush, which was rather dirty and had lost some of its bristles, though Joyce had brought it new just the other day, and sat down on the bed. She began to brush, gently teasing the tangled mat of hair apart. Mrs. Daniels began to repeat poetry, her speech much clearer than when she was just talking. Alice didn't understand much, but she loved the whole thing.

"Turning and turning in the widening gyre
The falcon cannot hear the falconer;
Things fall apart; the centre cannot hold;
Mere anarchy is loosed upon the world,

The blood-dimmed tide is loosed, and everywhere
The ceremony of innocence is drowned;
The best lack all conviction, while the worst
Are full of passionate intensity."

Leg stopped. "Like that one?"

"No," said Alice. "I don't understand it. But I don't mind." She went on brushing, still to the rhythm of the poetry.

Leg laughed. "Oh, well. Let's try this.

> *"Behind him lay the grey Azores,*
> *Behind the Gates of Hercules;*
> *Before him not the ghost of shores,*
> *Before him only shoreless seas.*
> *The good mate said, 'Now we must pray,*
> *For lo! The very stars are gone.*
> *Brave Admir'l, speak; what shall I say?'*
> *'Why say, "Sail on! sail on! sail on!"' '*

"—How's that?"

"Better." The last words gave her goose pimples. She didn't know why. "What's it about?"

" 'Bout Columbus. They taught you in school about Columbus, didn't they?"

" 'In fourteen hundred and ninety two, Columbus sailed the ocean blue,' " said Alice.

"Good. Well, he only made it because he sailed on and on even if he couldn't see what might lie ahead. Now, what do you think of this?—

101

> *"Well, did you hear? Tom Lincoln's wife today*
> *The devil's luck for folks as poor as they!*
> *Poor Tom! Poor Nance!*
> *Poor youngun born without a chance!"*

Alice brushed silently. She didn't know what she was supposed to make of it.

"Don't know what it means? Why, it's about Abraham Lincoln. He was born to such poor parents, it didn't seem as if he'd ever amount to anything. Remember when we were talking about handicaps?"

Alice purposely didn't nod.

"You don't like to hear that, do you? Well, what do *you* say?"

Alice was just waiting for that. She started off immediately.

> *"By the shores of Gitchee Gumee*
> *By the shining Big-Sea-Water,*
> *Stood the wigwam of Nokomis,*
> *Daughter of the Moon, Nokomis. . . ."*

She paused. That was the game. Mrs. Daniels took it up where Alice had left off.

> *"Dark behind it rose the forest,*
> *Rose the black and gloomy pine trees,*
> *Rose the firs with cones upon them.*
> *Bright before it beat the water,*
> *Beat the clear and sunny water,*
> *Beat the shining Big-Sea-Water.*

102

"Now, repeat it! *Dark behind it rose the forest . . .*"

Alice repeated it after Leg, line by line, then two at a time. By the end of every hair brushing she had four or five new lines in her head; sounds and pictures that shone out strange but clear against the dusty days.

"It's amazing how well you memorize," said Leg, swinging herself back in bed and relaxing with a sigh. "Are you sure you wouldn't like to try a different poem, though? That *Hiawatha* is so meaningless. How about:

"This thing I saw, or dreamt it in a dream . . ."

Alice shook her head violently. She didn't like that one. Leg was always trying to get her off Gitchee Gumee, for some reason. But Alice knew what she wanted.

"Oh, all ri'," As soon as Leg stopped repeating poetry, or talking about something unreal, she began to slur her words again.

Eventually Alice went to Mrs. Witherspoon's room. Mrs. Witherspoon, unfortunately, had recovered from her son's scolding and seemed herself again.

"You've certainly taken your time about coming," she said. "After all I've been through today. That wretched breakfast, and the nurse was so clumsy with my bath. Now, I want you to hunt up my old slippers, because these new ones are simply unbearable. But first, please try to do something about this terrible pillow."

Alice thought, How mean she must have been to her son when he was just a little boy. People were mean back and forth. You really had to feel sorry for both sides.

And she thought of what she'd said to Petrie, *she doesn't*

need you to hurt her too. How brave that had been of her! And he had acted so shocked.

When she had passed him in the hall later that day, he had looked at her, really looked at her and had given her a funny little wave. She brought that up to remember quite often.

But today she forgot it again right away, for as she passed the desk, she noticed that Nurse Boston was having a conference with Ray, whom they hadn't seen much lately, since she'd been transferred to First Floor. (What a relief!) But when Alice passed close to them, they stopped talking, which always made her very nervous. They must be saying something about her, but what could it be?

Alice remained uneasy for a day or two, but other things took her mind.

Leg was always after her. Usually waiting to tell her to do something. One morning she cried in a bossy tone, "I want a banana! I'm just like a pregnant woman, I have a food obsession. Get me a banana, Alice, without delay."

Alice gave a deep sigh.

"Don't repine," urged Leg. "Just go to the kitchen and get it. No problem. They always have them on hand."

"It's not allowed," said Alice, without hope.

"Aw, go on. Nothing's allowed till you try it . . .

"They are slaves who fear to speak
For the fallen and the weak . . .

You're not a slave, are you, Alice?"

Alice didn't like to say she was, though she felt like it, and she figured worse would happen if she continued to

104

stand there, so she went to the elevator, knowing she was on the moving belt of Leg's demands, and nothing could get her off except a disaster.

As she expected, the kitchen was teeming; lunch was being assembled. It was strictly against the rules to go through that door, on which hung a sign:

NO UNAUTHORIZED PERSONNEL

Maybe she could saunter, pretending to be authorized, into the storage cupboard and steal a banana.

While she was thinking over this scary idea, Browny came by, whistling as usual, wheeling a tray-carrier ready to load.

He stopped when he saw her. "What's up, Baby?"

She was too desperate to hesitate, even if Browny was a creep. "I want a banana."

"A banana?" She could see some kind of nasty joke crawling into his eyes, and hastily added, "For Mrs. Daniels."

"Oh! Mission Impossible, right? Well, here goes . . ." And he pushed his wagon on into the kitchen and was back in a moment with two bananas.

"Thanks," said Alice. She reached for the bananas.

"Is that all you gonna do to show your appreciation for my great help? 'Thanks'!" He said it in a high, squeaky voice, imitating her tone. "No chance. You gotta come through better than that!" And he puckered up his lips and made an exaggerated kissing sound.

Alice reached desperately for the bananas. Browny was tall and kept lifting them just out of her reach. She thought she would never get them, but one of the cooks yelled, "Browny! Come get your trays."

"OK, but you owe me," said Browny. He let the bananas go so suddenly that Alice staggered and almost fell. She didn't mind about that, just got her balance and rushed off, thankful for the bananas.

Leg was glad to get them, but not grateful. Next she wanted some fresh ice water.

Another day, she asked Alice to go to the library. Alice just stared. Where was this library?

"You don't know where it is?" For a wonder, Mrs. Daniels saw there was a problem. "It's not very far, but I don't know if I can direct you . . . I know, Ginger Man can show you. In fact, he could go for me, but it would be good for you to know where books come from."

Know where books come from! Well, for goodness sake. She wasn't that much of a dummy. And she wasn't going to just go up and speak to Ginger Man, either. She looked past Leg's left shoulder.

"Oh, boy, I know that look; you're digging in your heels, for what reason, I don't know." Leg spoke about her as if she weren't there. "Although perhaps I could guess."

She had her nerve to guess. Alice walked right out on her.

But during the break after lunch, when she usually went to her room for a nap, Alice was called for on the intercom. She was wanted on Second.

She knew what it would be about. Well, OK, then. She went on to her room, combed her hair carefully, and borrowed Francine's lipstick.

Ginger Man was walking Mrs. Daniels between her bed and her wheelchair.

Instead of screeching, "Oh-oh-oh-oh-oh!" like most patients in the same circumstances, or even giving out some Leg-like kind of thing like, "Take care! Watch out! Mind, now!" Leg was silent, except for harsh, heavy breathing; and Alice could see that Ginger Man had to work hard to help her stand upright and swing her legs, like a couple of boards. It wasn't walking, it was being walked.

"That's 'nuff," Leg said when she saw Alice, and Ginger Man boosted her back onto the bed, where she lay with her eyes closed. Ginger Man looked at Alice, pursed up his lips, and pointed from Alice to Leg, then noiselessly clapped his hands. Alice understood.

"How nice! You're walking!" Alice cried, sounding stiff to herself.

Ginger Man nodded vigorously.

"Books," said Leg faintly, without opening her eyes. "Told him go with you. Library."

Ginger Man nodded again.

"When?" asked Alice.

Ginger Man took the pad from his pocket and wrote on it.

FOUR O'CLOCK THIS AFTERNOON. LOBBY

Alice nodded too, very politely, so he would know that she understood. And that she agreed.

She did agree. It was scary, but it was all right. The touch on her cheek no longer burned in her memory. She and Ginger Man had become friends without her knowing it, through both of them being so anxious about Leg.

Ginger Man gave a little laugh, and nodded politely, just as she had—imitating her. But he was not being mean. It was just funny that they were standing there nodding for so

107

long. Alice laughed, too, and then went on down the hall, and he took the elevator back to Therapy. But Alice was not walking on the floor. She was walking in the air above it.

As she passed the desk, Nurse Boston called to her, with a commanding jerk of the head. "Alice."

Alice came down on the floor with a bang. Her heart dropped to the bottom of her stomach, even before the words were said.

"Alice, we've decided to transfer you to First Floor, and you can begin there tomorrow."

11

ALICE went to her room and lay down on the bed. It was her afternoon off, and she usually spent it sleeping, when she didn't work for someone else. She lay there a long time, not even hearing Francine come in.

"Alice?" said Francine, repeated without result, shrugged, grabbed her coat, and went out. Alice knew this was happening, but it was as if it were in some other place, concerning other people.

What was really happening was, they were taking her away from Leg. Though that in itself was very bad, worse was, it opened the door.

All the memories that were kept locked up came out. She couldn't stop them. She remembered the swing, and the sunny sky, and the apple tree; and Mama coming to the back door and calling.

"Alice!"

And when she went running, thinking it was a cooky, thinking it was love she was going to get, Mama stood up tall and looked down cold, and said, "Alice, you're going to have to go away for a while. I can't stand it any longer."

And they took her away that afternoon, and she never saw her mother again.

Then there were the memories of Willowstream, and of the lady who whipped her, and of the little children without any clothes on. They soiled their clothes (Alice hadn't done that for years), and then the people yelled at them and took their clothes off and left them. It was when Alice began to scream that the lady whipped her.

Then there was the visit when Daddy came and told her Mama had died. He cried and forgot about Alice and went away without saying goodbye.

All these memories went through her head not once but many times, and she seemed to be having to trace over them in black crayon so they would be there forever. She didn't want to, but she had to. It was as if she might have to know these things some day, like in a test, and if she failed she would be terribly punished. Even now she had forgotten some of it; even now she wasn't sure just how Mama had looked that last time. She got it mixed up with pictures and with stories.

Sometimes this went on for a very long time, and when she noticed the outside again, it was tomorrow. But this time the terrible, hurting round-and-round was broken into, suddenly, sharply. Alice tried to ignore the interruption, because she wasn't finished, she hadn't got to the other end, where it all went blank and she slept. But the interruption wouldn't go away. Finally she turned over and looked around to see if she could tell what it was.

It was nothing. Nobody was in the room. The corridor was quiet, except for Mrs. Googan screaming for her daughter, which happened so often that nobody even heard it.

Alice sat up feebly, trying to understand. What was going on? Where was she? Who was she? She wasn't ready to know.

But an answer came (from outside? from inside?): *Alice with golden hair!*

And then she knew what the interruption was. Mrs. Daniels. And she was supposed to meet Ginger Man at four o'clock. She looked at Francine's clock on the dresser. It was five minutes before four! (She suddenly realized that only a few months ago, at the Home, she hadn't known one time from another. But here, you had to know.)

Alice got up, her body still strange to her, her mind still cloudy, but clearing. What did a person wear to go to a library?

There wasn't much time, but fortunately her mind came to life very quick. She thought of the green sweater first—she'd never had a chance to wear it. And then she remembered that Mrs. Hones had brought her a yellow dress just the other day.

("You've got to have something decent to wear," said Mrs. Hones rather crossly. "And I know you have plenty of money. Just write me an authorization, and I'll get reimbursed by the bookkeeper. Isn't this a darling dress? I got it on sale, and it was only fourteen dollars."

Alice had pretended not to understand, looking her dullest, but Mrs. Hones had kept after her. "Come on, come on, I haven't got all day, write your name."

She held out a typed slip for Alice to sign.

"Fourteen dollars!" Alice objected. "That's too much." But she did like the dress.

"Oh, it is not! You know it."

"Anyway, I'd rather buy my own clothes."

"Well, next time maybe I can take you shopping. I just didn't have time. I've always got four times as much as I can fit into the day."

Of course, Alice had to sign, but she didn't say thank you, and she didn't say goodbye.)

. . . Anyway, now she was glad. First she slipped the yellow dress on over her uniform, she was in such a hurry, and when she tried to get it off again—for it didn't look good at all that way—it caught on a button. But at last she got the uniform off, and the dress on, and put on her sweater and combed her hair. The dress was like the soft yellow tissue paper the sweater had been wrapped in. It was nice. But she didn't have time to look very long, for it was two minutes after four.

Perhaps he would forget. Or think she wasn't coming. The elevator didn't come, getting diverted and sent down to the basement, as, waiting, she could tell from the arrow above the door. Alice felt hot nervousness creeping up her wrists and wondered in a panic if the nurse would open the door to the stairway for her.

Then it came.

He was waiting in the lobby. He couldn't have heard the elevator coming, but he was watching, and their eyes met, and they smiled. She knew from the way his eyes went up and down that he liked the yellow dress.

They went out and walked quietly down the walk. There was no other way, of course, except quietly. Alice didn't even think of starting a conversation, knowing he would have to stop and pull out his writing pad every time he answered. But she didn't mind. Talking was a bother. She en-

112

joyed looking around at the trees, which now were full of leaves, and at the flowers; and then she looked up at Ginger Man, who looked down at her; and then they smiled.

The library was about ten blocks.

Nobody minded.

Alice recognized the building, the flight of steps leading up to a corner entrance, and the large rounded windows. She had been taken to libraries from the home. (Did Leg think Alice had been living in a box?) But she had never liked them much. There were so many books that she could never read at all.

The young woman at the desk looked up, smiled, and said, "Oh, hello there, Jim! I'll go get Jerry."

She disappeared down a corridor of books, and when she came back Jerry was with her, a cheerful, skinny boy of about sixteen.

"Hi!" this boy said.

Then a strange thing happened. Ginger Man began to do finger plays. Long ago, some teacher had taught Alice songs with motions, and this was what it looked like, only much more complicated. Alice watched the dancing fingers with astonishment.

When the fingers stopped, Jerry answered with the same kind of antics, but he spoke out loud, too. "Sure, we must have those books. I'll hunt them up for you." He went back into the stacks.

The librarian said to Alice (though Ginger Man watched her lips, and then nodded), "Jim could find the books himself, with the numbers. But Jerry knows how to find them quicker. He and Jerry get a kick out of using sign language. Jerry's never been deaf himself, but both his parents are."

113

Jerry came back with an armload of books. "Any more, Jim?"

Ginger Man talked with his fingers again.

"OK." Jerry went off in a different direction and came back with one more book.

They said goodbye and started home.

This time Alice didn't look around so much. She had several things on her mind, and she frowned and looked at the sidewalk, trying to figure out what to do about them. She kept forgetting that she could talk to Ginger Man in the ordinary way, if he could just see her lips.

Finally he touched her shoulder very lightly so that she would look up at him, and then tipped his head inquiringly, and raised one eyebrow.

"Oh!" she said, remembering; and, forming the words distinctly, she said, "They've transferred me to First Floor."

Ginger Man made a sound. It was the first sound she had heard from him, except his laugh. It was a clicking of tongue against teeth, and it was just the kind of sound anybody might make, meaning, What a shame! How awful of them! What a mistake! Something has to be done about it!

They walked along some more, and occasionally Ginger Man would make that sound again, and she would look up, and they would exchange sorrowful and indignant glances.

Finally they reached the nursing home. Alice thought it looked much better in its wreathing of leaves, but she was sorry to see it, because it meant the walk was over, and Ginger Man would go downstairs and she would have to go upstairs. But there wasn't much room in her for being sorry, for she was all filled up with some wonderful feeling, like being happy, and like being safe.

At the door, Alice held out her hand for the books for Leg. She would take them up and tell Leg what had happened.

Ginger Man held them out but didn't let go of them. This was so he could keep her there while he gave her a comforting look, along with a combination of shake and nod of the head, while he raised one finger.

She knew perfectly what he meant. "Wait a little while. I'll fix it."

Still Alice held the books but didn't take them. There they were, reaching between the two of them, like a bridge. She must hold him till she could get some words said. What words did she need? She thought hard, then spoke slowly and clearly.

"Can I learn your language?"

They held the books together a moment longer. Ginger Man seemed to think hard a minute. Then he nodded. He didn't smile, but he looked glad.

12

ALICE took the books up to Leg, but she didn't tell about the transfer to First Floor. She didn't want Leg to pound her stick and holler. They paid no attention, in the nursing home, to patients hollering—unless the family was nearby. Ginger Man would take care of things.

"Good! Good!" said Leg. "Yes, here's *Accident,* by Eric Hodgins, and Margaret Bourke-White's *Autobiography.* And these others . . . That's great. We'll see what I can do with them. I knew that boy would find the right ones. He's a great boy."

She started reading right away and didn't even notice when Alice left.

But in the night, Alice got to worrying about not telling Leg about the transfer. When somebody else—that Ray, maybe!—showed up in the morning, would Leg think Alice had let them change her without even minding?

She decided to stop by on her way to first, and explain.

But how was she to explain? Leg would be sitting there waiting for her. Perhaps Leg would be in a good mood and would greet her with the verse that had the most meaning of all, bringing the two of them always so close together:

From my study I see in the lamplight
Descending the broad hall stair
Grave Alice and laughing Allegra
And Edith with golden hair.

And then Alice would have to say, "I'm not coming any more," and go away.

She couldn't do it.

Ray was waiting for the elevator when Alice got there. Alice pretended not to see her. It did no good.

"So you're promoted to First Floor?" said Ray. "That's great! You get so much more satisfaction out of working down there. The people know what's going on, and you can really do something for them. Poor me! I've got to take your place on Second."

She shook her head, sighing, but Alice didn't believe it. Ray wouldn't have moved if she hadn't wanted to; they must be giving her more money.

Ray got out at Second with a little wave.

Alice got out at First.

The charge nurse was sorry to see her. She looked up with a frown of annoyance. "Oh, yes, they told me they were sending you down today. Well, I'll get somebody to show you around."

Billy Lass was the person she got. Billy Lass was pretty, but she walked as if her muscles weren't quite tight enough to hold her bones, and her face looked the same way. Billy Lass was friendly, but Alice didn't like to have her around.

"Oh, you," said Billy Lass. "Well, anyway, I'm glad they shoved that spade."

After a bit, Alice realized she meant Ray.

117

"That know-it-all," muttered Billy Lass. "OK, here's the queen. She's another know-it-all." They went into a room where one old woman lay on a bed with her face turned away, and the other was reading a newspaper in an easy chair by the window.

"Mis' Rehner! Here's the new aide, replacing Ray."

"Good morning, my dear," said Mrs. Rehner. "I'm glad to meet you. I'm sure we'll get on splendidly together. I get along well with everyone. But what happened to that energetic colored girl who was here before—I can't think of her name?"

"Ray. They put her on Second. This here's Alice. Well, all right then, Mis' Rehner, Alice will be back when she's met the others."

"Who's that on the bed?" whispered Alice.

"Calanthrope. She's in despair," said Billy Lass with a giggle. "No use talking to her."

"Then why's she on First?" asked Alice.

"Money," said Billy Lass.

They went on down the hall, looking in at every room, though many were at moment unoccupied. "Guess she's in therapy," Billy Lass would say, or, "Mr. Jonas does woodwork. He's in the shop." Or, "Her daughter took her out to the beauty parlor. Maria isn't good enough for her."

But the patients they did find were mostly pleasant and took everything in, including Alice. Alice didn't feel at home with them. They looked her up and down, just like ordinary people who lived their own lives. They weren't like Suzy and most of the others on second, needing something from Alice.

But she found out by afternoon that the last was a mistake. They needed lots from her: errands, services, listening, only it wasn't really her they needed. Just somebody who could move about easily. In fact, by afternoon, Alice had decided it was particularly her they didn't need.

She had made so many mistakes. She got confused about who wanted the grape juice and who wanted pineapple; and she took Mrs. Rehner's mail to Mrs. Jacoby.

"I can't understand how you could make that error," said Mrs. Rehner when it had finally got straightened out. "Jacoby and Rehner bear not the slightest resemblance to each other."

"I just forgot which of you was which," Alice explained. But she learned instantly that her explanation was worse than her mistake.

"You confused *me* with Mrs. Jacoby?"

Mr. Piedmont's daughter visited, and Alice came into the room just in time to hear Billy Lass saying to them, "Oh, she's kind of a loony, but not at all dangerous."

And all the time, Leg and Mrs. Perciballi and Suzy were having to do without her.

Well, pretty soon Ginger Man would get it fixed. Of course, he couldn't do it today. He and Mr. Pitz worked in another nursing home on Wednesday. But tomorrow was Thursday, and he would have good news for her.

The patients on First Floor could get to therapy on their own, so Alice had no chance to see him in the morning. Nor at noon, for he ate in the dining room with the higher-type people: doctors and nurses and bosses. But she expected him at four, when the last therapy session ended.

So she was ready. She went to the desk to inquire after

119

the evening newspaper for Mrs. Rehner, though she had learned the day before that it didn't arrive till five.

"It doesn't arrive till five, I thought I told you that yesterday," said Mrs. Leaming. Her pleasantness wore off after lunch.

"Oh," said Alice, and turned away quickly, for Ginger Man had just come bounding up the stairs.

On account of Mrs. Leaming, Alice pretended not to notice him and strolled back into the corridor, where Ginger Man caught up with her.

When they were out of sight of the desk, Ginger Man handed her a note. As soon as he had watched her read it and received her nod and smile as if they were very important, he gave a little wave and ran down the stairs again. Mr. Pitz must be waiting.

The note said: MR PITZ SAYS SECOND FLOOR NEXT WEEK And it was signed, JIM.

She was glad it was signed Jim. Ginger Man was a play name.

The relief was so great that she went the rounds of the patients without paying much attention to what she didn't like about them, or worrying about what they didn't like about her.

She was getting used to them. They didn't wait eagerly for her, as Second Floor did; but they were getting used to her, too, and no longer seemed so tense and angry when she didn't understand right away.

But all the same, she reached toward Monday, she lived for Monday, and when it came, jumped out of bed with happiness. Nobody told her to make the change back, so she assumed she should go to Second on the same shift she'd had before; she turned up bright and early. First, of course, she went to Leg.

Leg was rummaging in her drawer. Her hair was wild and her nightgown was all pulled around. Her back was to the door.

Alice was about to cry out joyfully, "Mrs. Daniels, I'm back," when another idea came to her. She ran silently into the room and put her hands over Leg's eyes.

A great shudder went down Leg's body, and then she was rigid, and for a moment Alice was scared she would die. But then Leg spoke:

> *"A whisper and then a silence:*
> *Yet I knew by their merry eyes*
> *They are plotting and planning together*
> *To take me by surprise . . .*

"Are you just visiting, or have you come back to me?"

"I'm back!" cried Alice.

"Well! About time. That female jockey they put in your place is about to get me down. I told them they simply had to bring you back." Then she threw back her head and chanted:

> *"Do you think, O blue-eyed bandit,*
> *Because you have scaled the wall,*
> *Such an old moustache as I am*
> *Is not a match for you at all?"*

Alice stood and beamed. She didn't know should she say no or yes, but it wasn't a real question. She didn't know what a moustache had to do with it, but that didn't matter.

What mattered was that Leg was talking to her, that Leg's voice reached out and drew her into a world of knowledge and love, which she couldn't understand, but to which she belonged. She was the "blue-eyed bandit."

She thought of all the things she could do now for Leg, and the others, now she was back.

"Why Alice!"

Nurse Boston was at the door.

"Alice, you'd better get downstairs. You'll be late on your floor."

Breath, life, hope, all seemed knocked out of Alice. It couldn't be! Yet Nurse Boston, neat and firm and full of authority, must be right. Ray looked curiously over the crisp white shoulder. Alice knew they were both right, for some reason that had nothing to do with what she wanted, or Leg wanted, or any of the other patients wanted. But she would make one try:

"But Mr. Pitz said . . ."

"Oh, dear, I didn't know you were expecting— Well, yes, Mr. Pitz did say something about wanting you up here with some of his patients."

Leg cried, "Then she must be kept here! I demand it! Mr. Pitz is my doctor!"

"You know that Mr. Pitz is not a doctor at all," said Nurse Boston, firmer than ever after her momentary lapse. "It is the medical staff that decides what's best for the patients. Please get down to First, Alice."

It seemed as if she crackled as she turned away.

She didn't pay the least attention to Leg, who beat on the arms of her chair. "I demand! I demand!"

13

ALICE looked back at Leg.

The defiance wasn't gone from Leg's face, but the hope was. Leg would fight on, but Alice knew and Leg knew it was no use.

"Don't go!" Leg said hoarsely. "Don't let them take you away."

It was up to Alice.

"I won't," said Alice. "I'll be back." Leg really wanted her. Leg must have her.

She went out, trying to click her heels on the floor as Nurse Boston did. Once in the hallway, her courage collapsed, and she slowed down to a stop, looking straight ahead of her. What should she do? This was the best and the worst thing that had happened since her mother sent her away. Somebody wanted her, and they were being separated. And she couldn't do anything about it.

But she couldn't *not* do anything, either. But what?

Her finger poked the down button. Her feet took her into the elevator and out again. And down First Floor corridor to the desk.

"You're late, Alice!" said the nurse, looking pleased at

the chance to scold. Nurses did like to scold. Alice went walking right on. She could go to pieces and have a tantrum; or she could go back to her room and lose connection. But it wouldn't do any good. She had to think of something else.

"Well, here you are at last!" said Mrs. Rehner, and had a half a dozen things for Alice to do right away.

Alice did them, noticing with surprise that she was able to carry out orders she didn't even consciously hear. The morning paper; the beauty parlor appointment; the phone call to Mrs. Rehner's niece; the filter cigarettes. Mrs. Rehner had no complaints beyond the usual moaning, so Alice thought she must have things right.

She went on to the next patients.

By eleven, she had been over her route, and, amazingly, she had a plan. She went quietly down the back stairway (the only open one) to the therapy room.

Ginger Man was helping Miss Johnson over the stile, but he saw Alice.

He returned her look steadily for a moment, then helped Miss Johnson back to her wheelchair. The patients were lining up for the elevator to take them back to their floors for lunch.

Ginger Man came over to where Alice was waiting. He didn't pull the pad from his pocket. But she could tell from his sober face that he knew what had happened. Then why did he have nothing to say about it? Instead, he motioned to Mr. Pitz, who had just settled his last patient for the home trip.

"Oh, Alice!" said Mr. Pitz, with an air that seemed more jolly than was right. "I'm sure sorry about Second Floor. I laid it on thick, too, about how well you relate to the senile patients, and especially to Mrs. D., but you know how these nurses are—" He lifted his hands and let them drop discouragedly. "I'm just a hired man, to them."

"But—!" said Alice, and said it again, putting all the urgency in her body and soul into the one word, *"But—!"*

Mr. Pitz waited, as if for her to say more. Couldn't he understand? What he knew already? How important it was?

Mr. Pitz frowned. Maybe he didn't understand, or maybe he thought she was bugging him, or maybe he was mad because the nurses hadn't paid any attention to what he wanted.

"Oh, come on," he said roughly. "It really doesn't matter all that much. One day the patients say they'll die if they don't see you, and the next day they've forgotten who you are. Calm down."

He was shrugging out of his white jacket. "C'mon, Jim," he said. "I'm in a hurry. Come along if you want a ride."

Alice's eyes flew desperately to Ginger Man. Surely *he* wouldn't act as if it didn't matter . . .

He wasn't even looking at her. Alice couldn't believe it. He was dropping his white jacket on the chair and putting on his coat. He followed Mr. Pitz out without looking back.

Then, suddenly, she understood. Jim had given up. He couldn't do anything about it, and he knew he couldn't. How could he change things? He couldn't even speak. He was handicapped, and so he didn't even care.

Handicapped people usually couldn't do anything. So they didn't care. But she cared!

She hurried up the stairs, because she couldn't bear to wait for the elevator. There was one more thing she could try—Mrs. Hones; and the phone number was already in her mind. It was the kind of thing—like poetry—that she had no trouble remembering. In fact, forgetting was never her problem.

She went to the phone booth farthest from the office. She didn't want Mrs. Leaming to see what she was doing. Nice Mrs. Leaming, whom you couldn't trust at all. Alice dialed the number. She waited eagerly for that positive, unsympathetic voice.

But a different voice answered. Another kind of voice altogether, a young, light voice that scattered Alice's thoughts.

"Hello? Hello?" the voice kept saying. "This is Social Services, Miss Lopez speaking."

"Mrs. Hones?" Alice managed to ask.

"Oh, she's on vacation this week. Can I do anything for you? Can I give her a message?"

"No," said Alice faintly, and hung up. She was lost. She couldn't do it. She couldn't do what she had to do, not without help. So she might as well go off and go into herself for a while. That was all there was left.

Fortunately, everybody had gone to lunch. The patients who could make it were in the dining room, complaining over their food or slowly struggling to chew it up and swallow it. Alice could feel the effort that hung over the room like a great cloud. Mealtime was a disappointment, looked forward to but never much good.

The patients who were in their rooms were trying even more painfully and slowly to turn the Friday salmon and mashed potatoes (or the Kosher frozen plate) into strength enough so they could last a little longer. Some gave up and just sat there, not caring. A few impatient aides were trying

126

to shove spoonsful into loose old mouths, hurrying so they could get to their own lunch.

The rest of the staff were in their dining room, out of the way. That was good. Third floor corridor was empty as she reached for her doorknob. Just then Browny came swinging in through the laundry-stair door.

Alice was startled. Laundry-stair door was never opened. How could Browny come through like that? He saw her surprise and laughed. He held up a key and laughed again as he slid it into his pocket.

"They can't keep Browny out of anywhere he wants to go!" he bragged.

She thought, "That's true! Maybe Browny can help me. He's not handicapped."

"B-Browny," she said, stuttering over his name, for she had never tried to say anything that mattered to an orderly before. "C-can you help me?"

Browny stopped short. "What's the matter, Baby? You got trouble?"

Alice gave a sobbing sigh. "Yes, I have, Browny."

Browny looked at her some more, and then looked over her shoulder down the empty hall. "Well, let's us go into your room and talk it over, then!"

Suddenly they were in her room. He had hurried her in and shut the door behind them.

"They can't keep Browny out of anywhere he wants to go!" he repeated with leering emphasis.

Alice said hastily, "It's about Mrs. Daniels. It's about Second Floor . . . *Don't,* Browny! What are you doing?"

For Browny wasn't listening to her at all. Instead, he was coming toward her with a very queer expression—and

127

though she asked, and he didn't answer, she knew exactly what he was doing.

"You stop!" Alice said hoarsely, remembering all the things all the girls at all the schools had told her. "You stop or I'll scream!"

And she let her eyes go crazy. She wasn't sure she would be able to scream, but she could always let her eyes go crazy.

Browny's arms dropped to his sides, and he started back.

"Whew! Baby, what's wrong with you?" he muttered. And he held up his hands in front of him, as if he were afraid of her, or at least disgusted with her. "Never mind! I'll let you alone! Boy, will I let you alone!" And he got out of her room in no time.

Alice panted a little with relief and then opened her closet door. She was clearheaded now. At least Browny had kept her from going into that back wilderness where nothing could be done. She was leaving. She would take her yellow dress and her sweater—the rest didn't matter. This time she put her dress on over her uniform without caring how it looked; she didn't have any time to waste. They might try to keep her from leaving. But she'd just go home, and Dad would have to take her in. That was all that was left. She'd failed again.

She didn't know how to get home, but she would find out. Or, if she didn't, the police would find her and return her to her father, as they had done when she was small and had tried to run away from Willowstream.

She rode the empty elevator clear to the basement, where she followed Miss Johnson's escape route. She met no one.

It all went perfectly. She just walked out and down the

drive. She had done that well, she thought. She had learned a lot at the home. What a shame she had to go away. She could probably learn some more. And she thought of the sign language, but that made her angry. He's handicapped, she thought scornfully.

She tried not to remember the last time she had gone walking—with Jim, to the library. This day was not like that one. That one had been beautiful, full of light and happiness. Today, though summer now had fully come, the green was dark and hot, and the red zinnias bright as paint beside purple ageratum and yellow marigolds. She didn't like them.

It took her a while to find the hospital—she followed almost the same clumsy procedure she had before. But this time she knew she had found it once and could find it again —and there it was. She went up the steps, crossed the lobby, and found the rank of public phones.

It was dim in the phone booth till she remembered to pull the door shut, and then the light went on, and she looked up her father's name. It took a long time. First she had to find the M's. Then McMartin. Then Rufus. 423 Quade Ave. That was the new address.

She went out and asked the girl at the desk how she could get to Quade Ave.

The girl looked hard at her. Alice thought for a minute someone from the nursing home had called, trying to find her. She expected the girl to say, "You ran away from the nursing home," or "You're retarded." But she didn't. She said, "I beg your pardon?"

Alice told her the whole address. "Where is it?"

"Oh, that's clear across town. Well, you turn right at the corner—do you have your car?"

Alice shook her head, trying not to smile. The idea, that she might have a car!

"You could get the Number Eight bus on the corner right outside," said the girl. "Get off at Tenth St. Get the driver to tell you."

Alice thanked her. The girl was now looking at her in a really puzzled way, and Alice noticed that her dress, with the uniform under it, did look rather lumpy. But she held her head high and marched out, and nobody stopped her.

She asked a kind old lady where to take the bus, and the kind old lady told her wrong. After six busses had passed, and no Number Eight, she asked a man, who told her it was on the other side. She gathered a handful of change, and when Number Eight came, and she got on, she held the money out so the driver could take what was needed. He looked at her curiously, but *she* thought it was a smart thing to have done.

Riding down Palisade, she was tired but sort of happy. She'd done so many things she'd never done before, and never thought she could do.

The bus driver told her to get off at Tenth and walk to Quade.

She started walking very fast and hopefully down Tenth, found Quade, and turned right. This was a dingy street, walled in with tall, gloomy houses set close together. Her heart was beating hard.

Maybe she should have phoned first. But if she'd phoned, maybe they wouldn't have let her come. Besides, nobody was home in the day time, everybody was out working.

The four hundred block—467 . . . 453 . . . 449 . . . 437 . . . 423.

130

There. It was like all the others, a kind of dark purple wooden house that seemed to have been shoved into a space too small for it. It looked closed, locked, deserted. But it was her house. In a way.

If nobody was home yet, she would just sit on the steps and wait.

She rang the bell, looking down at the dusty square of carpet that lay there for wiping your feet. She almost thought she recognized those stiff roses, though they were so faded and worn. Maybe this ragged little square had been cut out of the old carpet in the living room. And the rocking chair on the porch—could that have been the chair Mama rocked her in? No. No. It didn't *feel* the same. That one had arms that sometimes hit your head. It had a big lap, though, that old one, and wide rockers, and swayed so comfortably when someone sang to you, "Rockabye baby, in the tree top."

The door opened.

Alice was shocked that someone was there after all, and still more shocked when she looked into the face of the woman. This was a person she had never seen before, someone so unfamiliar that it seemed totally wrong for her to be there.

"Oh—" Alice didn't know what to say. She thought hard. Then said, "I was looking for the McMartins. Do they live somewhere around here?"

The woman nodded.

"Sure do. Right here. I'm Mrs. McMartin, myself. What can I do for you?"

14

Mrs. McMartin! The first shock was so great it made Alice's head whirl. Then she examined the woman very carefully. The round face, the tight waves of very black hair, the piercing dark eyes and red cheeks. There was no McMartin about her. McMartins were all tall and slim, either mousy-brown, like Dad and Ernie, or yellow-haired, like Mama and Carol and Alice.

"You can't be," she said firmly. "I'm Alice."

The round placid face tensed up right away. Alice recognized that look. The woman knew who Alice was, all right.

"Oh. Alice. Well, come on in; it's time we got acquainted. I told Rufus he should tell you we were getting married, but it all came up so sudden."

Alice followed the woman through a dark hall into a sudden burst of sunshine—a dining room, lighted from the back window at the west. The window was full of plants, and the neat furniture was decorated with tidies and knickknacks.

Alice looked from one thing to another. It had been a long time since she was home, and of course the family had

132

moved several times since they lived in the original house that had been her real home. But there had always been furniture that she recognized to make her know that she really had once lived in a home that—partly—belonged to her. Here, there was nothing.

The woman watched with narrowed eyes. "Sit down, Alice. I know you're shocked at not seeing the old things around. They're up on second floor, in the apartment we rent out now. You see, I was your father's landlady, he and the kids lived upstairs. But when Carol lit out a few weeks ago, the poor man was so lost—well, I'd been thinking about it, anyway. I've been needing a man around the house. My Timothy died four years ago. Well, anyway, your dad and I got married, and he moved down here. It's working out real nice."

"Carol's gone? Where?" asked Alice faintly. Everything had changed. It didn't make any real difference to her, but still she hated having things change—and having them get further and further away from the time when she had had a part in them.

"Who knows?" The new Mrs. McMartin shrugged. Alice could tell that she didn't care for Carol at all. "Ernie still sleeps in the little room on third floor. He's no trouble. . . . Well, could I get you a cup of tea or something? Or coffee? Or milk?"

"I'll take the tea," said Alice.

She was sitting in a big overstuffed chair with a crocheted tidy on the back, facing toward the TV in the corner. It was a pretty big room, dining and living room combined, rather crowded with the living room chairs and sofa, and the large dining table, straight chairs, and sideboard. The double doors at one end were curtained, and Alice decided the bedroom must be there.

Where was the glass-front china closet that Mama had kept her collection of small china dolls in? Alice didn't like to think of strangers handling them.

Mrs. McMartin brought Alice a tiny embroidered napkin, a nice white plate, and a delicate flowery teacup with a teabag floating in the hot water. Then she passed homemade sugar cookies.

"I must say, you're a prettier girl than your sister," she said. "Nicer disposition too, I bet. Say, that makes me think! Come in here a minute."

She opened the double doors, disclosing, as Alice had supposed, a bedroom, with a massive unfamiliar bed and dresser. Over the bed hung a solemn-faced photograph— the dead Timothy, Alice thought. But Mrs. McMartin pointed to another wall.

"Just look at that!"

It was the well-known photo, or rather, blown-up snapshot, of Mama and Alice, when Alice was about five. Alice knew it well, but she gasped, now, when she saw it again after such a long time. Because it was not the baby who was Alice, it was the mother, with her wide-spaced eyes and timid smile, showing separated front teeth.

"Oh, my!" said Alice.

"Yes!" said Mrs. McMartin. "You see it too, don't you? You're the living image of her."

So like, and yet—Alice thought again, in protest this time. So different. For Mama had been wonderful.

"Well, I'll call up your father," said Mrs. McMartin "He

134

should hurry home from work to see you. You can stay for dinner, can't you?"

She didn't wait for an answer, but bustled off to the kitchen.

Alice looked at the picture of her mother again before following back to the living room. Poor mother, her place was filled up, now. The house was filled up. There was no place in it for Mama, nor of course for Alice either; not even the little tiny spot among familiar things she had hoped might be there.

"He'll be right home," said Mrs. McMartin, coming back. "Well, let's sit and talk and enjoy ourselves while we wait. I'm really glad you came. I've felt real bad about not getting in touch, but you know your father—it takes him a long time to get around to things. He was so upset about Carol running off like that. Well, anyway, Ernie's a nice boy. And I think you and I are going to get along fine. Do they let people visit you any time at that place where you work? You must have some time off?"

"Yes . . ." said Alice, letting her voice trail off. She didn't really know. She'd never asked to get off, except sometimes when she slept a free afternoon away. There was nowhere for her to go so she'd mostly filled in for other people when she was off.

"Oh well, we can find out," said Mrs. McMartin. "Why, here's your dad already!" The doorbell was ringing. "Must've forgot his key."

She hurried out, closing the hall door behind her. So as to have a word with dad first, Alice thought.

But then she heard another woman's voice. Alice started up nervously. Had somebody come to take her back? She seemed to recognize the voice, but how would they have known where she was? Would they be angry at her? She wondered if she could slip out the back way, but before she could make up her mind, Mrs. McMartin ushered in Mrs. Hones. Oh! Of course, *that* voice. But Mrs. Hones was on vacation! How could she be here?

"You're on vacation," said Alice.

"How can I have a vacation, you little pill?" said Mrs. Hones, but she was smiling. She was pretending it was funny. She was doing that for the benefit of Mrs. McMartin.

"I couldn't stay there, because they switched me to First Floor," said Alice.

"But First Floor's easier!"

Alice shook her head. "Mrs. Daniels," she said.

Mrs. Hones looked at her wonderingly. "Who would ever have thought it?" she said slowly.

"Will you have a cup of tea?" asked Mrs. McMartin. "Then you can tell me what this is all about."

"Fine. I guess I'd better," said Mrs. Hones.

When Mrs. McMartin brought the tea, in another pretty cup, this one blue laced with gold (Alice was proud of it before Mrs. Hones), she said briskly, "You mean Alice ran away?"

"Seems like it," said Mrs. Hones. "How about it, Alice?"

Questions, questions. What was she to answer? She thought of Ginger Man's flying fingers and wished she had a language, too. But if she did nobody would understand it. Because more than words were missing.

How could she make them understand? About Leg's face —strong old features drawn with pain, which always relaxed into friendly amusement when Alice came in . . .

The busy strut of Ray, and Nurse Boston's cold annoyance . . . The greedy sly face of Browny coming toward her . . . And—but she wouldn't think of that now—the way Jim had seemed to wither up and fade away when he couldn't help.

To put it all together and explain why she ran away!

She could only despairingly gaze into Mrs. Hones's dark brown eyes, silently begging her to understand and explain.

"Well, she's not in any trouble," said Mrs. Hones, after what seemed a very long, considering silence. "The nursing home is just worried about her, and sorry she ran off. The only thing they could tell me was that this transfer from one floor to another seemed to upset her terribly. She should have been pleased, for they took her off Second, where the patients are mostly senile and difficult and need heavy care, to First, where they're all ambulatory and in pretty good shape mentally. Alice, why did you mind so much?"

"Leg," said Alice.

"And that's *it?* It's incredible," Mrs. Hones said, turning to Mrs. McMartin. "Here's this really difficult old lady— chronic brain syndrome, strokes and what-not—and she and Alice get along famously. I think the staff decided the woman was monopolizing Alice's time, and maybe Alice was encouraging her to demand too much. That could make it hard for the nurses. That it, Alice?"

How did she know what it was? Alice wouldn't look at Mrs. Hones. She couldn't see over other people's walls; she didn't have to let them see over hers.

"Here comes her father," said Mrs. McMartin, tensing up again, as she had at first. She pushed her head out toward Mrs. Hones like a tortoise looking out of its shell and sort

137

of hissed, "Whatever's wrong, she can't live here. I don't want her father even to know why she came. He hasn't had a real home, you might say, ever."

She and Mrs. Hones looked at each other for a minute, hard.

"OK," said Mrs. Hones. "We'll just have to find another solution. This wouldn't have been too good for Alice, anyway. We'll go in a minute."

So the meeting with dad was just a hello and goodbye in the dark hall.

15

THEY DROVE away from the house. Alice said nothing. Mrs. Hones finally broke the silence.

"You do realize that I have to take you back?"

"Yes," Alice answered absentmindedly, for her thoughts had been busy for some time with another thing. "You have my folder—do you remember what's in it?"

"Your folder? You mean your case record? Yes, I guess I do. Why?" Mrs. Hones was driving more slowly, looking at Alice out of the corner of her eyes. Alice knew she would have to be careful if she expected to get an answer. Mrs. Hones was so cagey about telling her anything about what was in that folder.

"Mrs.—that woman—showed me a picture of my mother. I saw it before, but not for a long time. She looked like me."

"Oh?" said Mrs. Hones. Her voice sounded careful. Alice felt a warning in it. She thought of the pits covered with branches that animals crash into and are caught . . . But she had to go on.

"Was she like me?" asked Alice.

The silence went on for a long, long time. Alice guessed

the answer from the silence; and Mrs.—that woman—had said, 'He hasn't had a home, you might say, ever.' (But that wasn't true. Alice could remember.)

"They didn't do so much testing in those days, Alice," said Mrs. Hones finally. She waited for Alice's next question. But Alice couldn't ask it. Now that it was right in front of her, she couldn't risk knowing the answer. She would walk around the pit and never come back to this dangerous spot again.

And now they were pulling up before the nursing home. They went in. Maria craned her neck. Mrs. Leaming looked up without expression; it was a different face without the smile.

"Bell in?" asked Mrs. Hones casually.

"He certainly is," said Mrs. Leaming.

He certainly was. He sat behind the broad desk and watched them come in. He leaned back in his swivel chair and swayed a little, but said nothing as they moved step by step, a lot of steps, across the floor.

"Alice has something she would like to say to you," said Mrs. Hones.

Alice's heart gave a great lurch, and she turned a panicky look on Mrs. Hones. She couldn't tell it herself! What should she say? Groping back along the dark passage of hours, she recalled that her wanting to be with Leg seemed to be what they didn't like, so she ought not to mention it.

"Browny scared me," she said.

"What's that? What are you talking about?" Mr. Bell's chair snapped forward. "How did Browny get into this? What's she talking about, Mrs. Hones?"

"I don't *know,*" said Mrs. Hones. "Good heavens, she

never mentioned that at all. She's a little confused by all the turmoil. I should tell you that when she got to her father's house, she found he had married in the last few weeks without ever letting her know."

"Well, that figures," said Mr. Bell.

"But what she told me, and I'm convinced it's the truth, was that she simply wanted to take care of the patients on Second Floor. It's not unnatural, really. She's been with them ever since she came. And I think the floor staff would bear out my impression that she was doing a very good job there."

"Too good," said Mr. Bell, nodding with his lips pursed up—which made "too good" turn into "too bad." "Interfered with the routine, with discipline."

"With *discipline?*" repeated Mrs. Hones, almost before the word was out of his mouth.

It hung between the two of them. Alice saw it. Her head cleared, for now she was out of the picture. Now they were mad at each other. She was relieved, and quite interested.

"Well, perhaps an unfortunate choice of words," said Mr. Bell. "You know quite well what I mean. There has to be order, and the patients have to follow the medical plan set up for them, even if they don't happen to like it. It's a very important for the aides to understand this—especially on Second Floor."

"Yes, that is important, of course," said Mrs. Hones, but her tone (like Mr. Bell's, before) made the words mean the opposite. "But the Institutional Care Division that employs me considers it important not just to keep the patients alive, but to keep them as happy as possible. If I see them unhappy, it's my duty to report it."

141

"Really! Well, we all have a duty to inform the state department when we see deficiencies in their employees," said Mr. Bell. He rang the bell for Mrs. Leaming. "Why don't you talk to Nurse Boston about it? I'm sure that will settle your mind."

Alice tiptoed out after Mrs. Hones, hoping not to divert the irritation to herself. Mrs. Hones's brows were drawn down, and her lips folded in tight.

"See that? I'm in hot water again," said Mrs. Hones. (She swept past Mrs. Leaming's inquiring face without a word.) "And all because of you. Why in the world didn't you speak your piece to Mr. Bell like you did for me? What's all that about Browny?"

Alice wouldn't answer about Browny. "What are you going to do now?"

"Oh." Mrs. Hones gave a huge sigh. "I'll have to talk to Boston. I've got a little in with her. I can probably get you back on Second. But you may have lost me my job. Imagine that jerk saying, 'we all have a duty to inform the state department!' I know a few things about him he wouldn't like them to know."

Vague memories drifted through Alice's mind. People were always saying things about Mr. Bell. *I don't believe he really gives them their allowances . . . He lets the doctors get their pay when they don't even come—must get a rake-off . . .*

Well, she couldn't worry about things like that. And she wasn't concerned about Mrs. Hones's job. Mrs. Hones could take care of herself. And she could take care of Alice, too. Alice flew to the elevator, and then down the hall to Leg.

Leg's first action was negative. She was lying flat on her

back when Alice looked in, but she was awake. She couldn't help being awake because her roommate, old Mary Symes, was yelling.

"Nu-urse! Nu-urse! I'm dying! I need my laxative! I haven't moved my bowels in a week! I'm dying! Nu-urse!"

Leg jerked upright in bed and grabbed her stick. She began to pound on the floor.

"Stop that, you idiot! They gave you a dose yesterday, and you moved your bowels today! You're not dying, unfortunately. Shut up and let me get some sleep."

Her stick slipped from her hand, and as she leaned painfully to reach for it, she caught sight of Alice.

"Well, so you finally came back, did you?"

"Could I brush your hair?" asked Alice.

"Now? It's late afternoon! You're too late by hours—days. Maybe tomorrow." And Leg lay down and closed her eyes.

But Alice knew how Leg was.

She went on up to Third, ignoring curious glances. Everybody knew she'd run away, but it didn't matter. She was back. Only it wasn't the same. Why did she have this low, empty feeling?

Then she remembered: Ginger Man. She'd found out he wasn't really any good. Just another handicapped person.

Nobody said a word to Alice about her having run away. Nurse Boston did greet her next morning, though, instead of just nodding.

"Glad you're back on our floor, Alice. By the way, you might take a little extra pains with Mr. Burket. He doesn't seem quite himself this week."

Alice ran into Mr. Burket's room and patted him and

143

told him she'd be back soon. Then on to Leg. And Leg was ready with the hairbrush. It looked more disreputable than ever.

"Joyce brought me a new one," Leg said, "but somebody stole it. This thievery is getting intolerable."

Alice settled herself on the edge of the bed, braced Leg's back with a pillow, and started brushing.

Leg started the poetry.

> *"My life is cold, and dark, and dreary;*
> *It rains, and the wind is never weary;*
> *My thoughts still cling to the mouldering past,*
> *But the hopes of youth fall thick in the blast*
> *And the days are dark and dreary.*

"—like that?"

"No!" said Alice.

"Quite right, too. But it's by your favorite Henry Wadsworth Longfellow. And listen to the next stanza:

> *"Be still, sad heart! and cease repining;*
> *Beyond the clouds is the sun still shining;*
> *Thy fate is the common fate of all,*
> *Into each life some rain must fall,*
> *Some days be dark and dreary."*

"But not all," said Alice. "Not all days."

"Oh, right, not all!" cried Leg. "You came back, didn't you? And . . .

"I have you fast in my fortress
And will not let you depart,
But put you down in the dungeon
In the round-tower of my heart!"

"Now me," said Alice, and began immediately,

"By the shores of Gitchee Gumee . . ."

Leg let her go through it, but when Alice paused for the next lines, Leg said, "No more now. We haven't time. There's something more important we've got to do first."

"What?" asked Alice apprehensively.

(She remembered the last important job Leg had stuck her with. "I'm going to write a book," Leg had announced. "But I'll need a typewriter." She had sent Alice everywhere to try to borrow, buy or beg a typewriter. When this failed, Leg had forced her son to bring her one.

"But Mother," he said when he brought it, "I don't see where we're going to put it? Where will you work?"

"Alice will find me a table," said Leg calmly.

And Alice actually had, after many agonies and setbacks; but by that time someone had stolen the typewriter.)

So now Alice said nervously, "What have I got to do?"

"Why, it's you and Appolonia," said Leg severely. "The idea of the two of you being on such bad terms. Appo looked after me a lot before you came, and still drops in to pass the time of day. She talks a lot of nonsense, but she's really intelligent and honest and kind. You two ought to be friends. So I'm going to bring you together."

"But she doesn't like me," said Alice.

"But she says you don't like her," said Leg.

And I don't, Alice thought. She didn't want to have anything to do with Appolonia and always went the other way when she saw Appolonia's proud figure marching down the hall. She never cared to meet those sharp glinting eyes.

So her heart sank, but she said nothing more, because she knew it was no use, Leg would carry through, would at least make the effort, no matter what Alice said. Alice would just have to live through it.

It happened the next day.

Pan poked her head in Mr. Beidenheim's door, where Alice was hearing about Mrs. Beidenheim while giving him his lunch.

Pan said, "The dentist is here, and Leg can't find her plate. She says maybe you could help."

Alice finished Mr. Beidenheim's spinach rather too fast, turning back the tender tales with sloppy green mouthfuls, and sped up the hall. If the dentist could fix the plate a little so Leg could wear it without getting a sore on her gums, she could talk clearer. Alice hated not being able to understand her sometimes.

But when she got to the room, the dentist was not there: Appolonia was there.

Appolonia looked startled when she came in. Then she looked mad. "You sneak!" she said, turning on Leg. "You weren't waiting for the podiatrist at all—only her!"

"Right," said Leg calmly. "Now come here, Alice. You two have got to make up. What's wrong with you, anyway? What makes you so mean about her, Alice? She stood up for you with Mr. Bell, when you let Miss Johnson get away.

146

You know that, don't you? Yet you snubbed her when your family came and didn't introduce her to them."

Alice skipped that part. She didn't want to think of it. She muttered, "She called me a dumb crumb."

"So she did," said Leg. She turned to Appolonia and scolded her. "How could Alice be a dumb crumb? If a crumb is dumb, then it isn't really a crumb, is it? She didn't mean to hurt your feelings. She just didn't know how to cope with her family's prejudice."

"Oh, I know she isn't really responsible; I just don't have any time for her." Appolonia stood up and gave it to Leg, she gave it to her good. "You know my plans. I'm going to get training in some health field—podiatry or something—and stick with the care of the aged. That's enough for one black uneducated pickaninny to take onto herself. I'm not about to set up a counseling service for high-grade morons at the same time. So goodbye."

And she strode out.

Alice looked accusingly at Leg. "See," she said. That was exactly what she'd thought, though she couldn't have said it in words. Appolonia's proud march and hard eye told her, every time she saw them, that Appolonia had no time for her.

"Oh, brother," said Leg. "Well, for the time being, I'm beat. But I'm mad at both of you."

She sulked for two days. But on Monday, something new. She couldn't wait even till Alice got into the room before she shouted, "Did you hear 'bout all those burglaries over the weekend?"

Alice nodded. Everyone had. The constant trickling away of patients' belongings—candy, perfume, tobacco, maga-zines—had suddenly stepped up. Over the weekend—a time

147

for visitors, unprogrammed and understaffed—TV sets had disappeared from second and third, cash from Social Security checks, and a large amount of linen from the laundry.

"Well, I've had enough of it. Know what I'm going to do?" Leg demanded.

Alice gaped. Was Leg planning to join the police?

"It's not that these poor creatures—aides, orderlies, whatever—who're doing it, probably with accomplices from outside making use of them. It's not that they're really bad people," said Leg. "It's that they don't realize what they're doing. They don't understand the choices. Nobody has ever given them a chance, really explained things, opened up their minds! So, I'm going to give a class in ethics. That means, not stealing. Let's see, how shall we set it up?"

16

ALICE stared at Leg nervously.

She didn't feel called on to give an answer. Leg would do that herself. It was only that Alice would have to carry out whatever Leg decided on.

Alice thought this was the worst plan Leg had ever had.

Certainly the stealing was awful. It gave Alice the creeps. Even though nobody had ever spoken to her about it—of course, nobody ever spoke to her about anything, except to give her orders or make silly jokes—she did manage to pick up rumors. The latest rumor was that somebody had seen a truck standing at night outside the open laundry door.

Everyone was jumpy, all the aides and the orderlies and even the nurses. Either they guessed who it was and were afraid to tell, or they didn't guess who it was and half suspected each other; or else, of course, they were guilty and terrified of being found out. Alice could imagine how those guilty people would feel, sick in the stomach and constantly watching for signs of suspicion. Alice felt guilty like that without having done a thing. So Alice, like Leg, was sorry for them. She hadn't had anything stolen, herself, for she kept her money in the safe in the office, and she didn't have anything else worth stealing.

"Well, let's see," said Leg, getting on with her plan. "First, of course, we'll have to get out a flyer."

"How?" asked Alice.

"If they hadn't stolen my typewriter, I could cut the stencil myself," bragged Leg. "But if they hadn't stolen my typewriter, I might not even have been goaded into devising my plan. Mrs. Leaming will have to cut the stencil."

"Oh, no!" said Alice. "Mrs. Leaming doesn't like to do extra things." She had been ordered to ask Mrs. Leaming for writing paper, library books, stamps, and innumerable other things, and she knew.

"You're implying that she's lazy," said Leg, adding severely, "If you had to carry around eight hundred pounds on a couple of wet noodle ankles, you would be, too. Well, then, we'll ask Maria."

"Oh," said Alice, with a discouraging drop to her tone. Discouraged was more like it. Alice tried always to stay clear of Maria. It wasn't exactly that she didn't like her, but Maria was always trying to take her over.

"Want me to fix your hair this afternoon, Beautiful?"

If Alice didn't say no very firmly, she knew Maria would throw the apron over her instantly and fix her hair however Maria thought fit. She might cut it or curl it or braid it very tight; which was not Alice's idea of how golden hair should be treated.

Or Maria would call out, "Why don't you come over on your break and try some of this weaving? It's real fun. You could make presents for your family."

Alice didn't feel the need to make presents for her family,

and besides, none of the other aides did it. The craft shop was for the patients, and Alice didn't like to be treated as if she were one of them.

Maria didn't understand Alice's standoffishness. "Why don't you like Maria, Kid?" she asked once as if she really minded. "Maria likes you fine."

But Maria had been watching when Alice's family visited and Appolonia passed by, an incident by which Alice felt mysteriously downgraded.

So Alice hated to make a request of Maria, but there was no way out. Leg wouldn't let up on her till she'd done it.

Before Alice could tell Maria what she was after, Maria called out to her and said, "Good, you finally coming to let Maria do your hair? Look, I found a picture of how it would look very good." And she rummaged in her drawer till she found a clipping of a girl from a magazine. The hair was golden, and it looked lovely. Not curled tight or cut short, but floating free, just the way Alice always wished for.

"How do you get it that way?" she couldn't help asking.

"Big rollers," said Maria. "I do it now?"

Alice shook herself loose from this daydream. It didn't matter any more how she looked anyway. "Mrs. Daniels wants you to make up some flyers for her," she said shortly.

"Sure. I can do them on the multigraph. What about?"

Alice handed over Mrs. Daniels's copy, which Leg had printed herself, painfully but legibly.

ETHICS FOR AIDES. SIX SESSIONS, ROOM 238

7:30 P.M.

ALLEGRA DANIELS, TEACHER

"Hey! What you got here? What in the world is this? What does it mean?"

151

"Leg wants to give a class in not stealing," said Alice.

Maria's black eyes widened, and she crossed herself. "Oh, that old lady is crazy," she whispered. "Not that I don't like her a lot," she added quickly. (Maria claimed to like everybody, which made you wonder.) "You go tell her Maria says no. Tell her she best mess out of this business. I, Maria, have never, not ever had anything to do with the Italian gangsters, nor my family, for we are not that kind of people. But I hear about it all my life, and I know better than to mingle in any part of stealing—neither steal, no, nor try to keep anybody else from stealing, me, no. Tell her that," she ended positively, and then frowned at Alice, though not crossly.

"I tell her myself," she said.

Alice let her go. She went to fetch the *New York Times* for Mr. Burket. Though he seldom read it any more, he seemed to like to have it near him.

When she got back to Leg, she was greeted by fireworks.

"They're trying to stop me!" Leg cried furiously. "They're trying to hush me up! Well, that they can't. You run down and tell Ginger Man I've got to see him right away."

"No," said Alice.

Leg glared. "Well, you will so do it! What's this with you and Ginger Man? He told me you were mad at him. He feels bad about it."

"I haven't got time," said Alice and walked out. She couldn't bear to go to Ginger Man. It was bad enough to see him glance at her when she took Miss Johnson down; as if he didn't know what had happened!

But of course, Leg just got somebody else to go to Ginger

Man, and the next day she showed Alice a sheaf of nicely printed notices—Ginger Man's printing.

Ginger Man had not tried to stop Leg's plan. Perhaps he was somebody after all.

But maybe he just didn't realize that this was a dangerous thing. He was an outsider. He came and went, and spent only eight to ten hours a week in the nursing home. Things like the stealing scare wouldn't sink in, especially since he couldn't hear anything and couldn't really tell what was going on. No matter what "third language" Leg said he had. He was a poor thing, and Alice didn't need him.

But she read his flyers. They were changed from Leg's.

PUBLIC RELATIONS COURSE FOR AIDES
ALLEGRA DANIELS, LECTURER

"Look!" Alice cried, underlining the words, "public relations," with her finger.

"Yes," said Leg comfortably. "He's a mighty clever lad. He knew they'd go for that. I wonder if there'll be room enough here for them all."

She worried about were they would sit, but Alice worried about how Leg would feel if nobody came. Alice was wrong. Everybody came.

Appolonia came—well, that was out of liking Leg. Francine came, bright-eyed, to find out still more stuff about the aged. Jacques Ben Prince came, smiling out of the corners of his eyes at Appolonia; and Petrie came and stood sternly with his arms crossed. Browny came—Alice pretended not to see him—and Pan came and Billy Lass, chattering, and everybody else. There were quite a few whom Alice still couldn't connect up with the right names. They all came!

153

"I'm gwat—gratified to see you all," said Leg. She was propped up in bed, but had been too excited all day to let anybody comb her hair or bathe her, so she looked terrible. "Now we'll get down to business. I wonder who would like to define 'public relations'?"

Petrie stepped forward. "I would," he said. "Well, we come here tonight on account of we do respect you, Mrs. Daniels. But you're in over your head. Public relations to you don't mean nothing but stealing, and you got some plan about it, and you in too deep. Better let us work things out ourselves."

Leg clapped her hands. "Right! You're exactly right!" she cried. "I'm proud of you, My faith in you all is justi—justified. The course really is in 'not stealing,' as you say. I guess 'honesty' is a more positive way to put it. And you do have to solve it yourselves. I think the very first thing to be done is for the thief to confess."

She let the startled silence last for a few moments, looking with interest from one tense face to another.

"Now, I'm not going to ask you to confess openly, that would be too difficult and humiliating. As soon as the thief —or thieves—make their statement, that part of the matter must be forgotten.

"Then we can turn away from this painful aspect of the problem and begin the real, thoughtful, thrilling study of honesty, which can make all of us better and happier people."

The tension held. Leg's words floated without any effect past the tight anxiety on every face. But she swept on.

"So, for tonight, I suggest that everybody just write some-

154

thing on a small piece of paper—you can tear up this old notebook, Alice, and distribute the slips; make them all the same size—then you can fold your slip and give it back to me. You can write 'lamb chops for dinner,' if you want to, if you have nothing to confess. But if everybody writes, and everybody turns in a slip, the anonymity of the culprit is preserved. I promise you, if the thievery ceases, and the booty is returned, nobody but me will ever know."

"Mrs. Daniels, you're out of your mind," said Appolonia. "You're playing with trouble; at least, wasting your time." She gave a wide despairing gesture. "Oh, what can I say?" She scribbled on her slip, and when Alice passed the bowl, dropped it in.

In uneasy silence, the others did the same.

"The next session will be next Tuesday, same time," said Leg. "You stay, Alice, and help me get rid of the incriminating evidence."

The others left, as if they could hardly wait to go, yet with uneasy backward glances. Alice wished she could leave. But she couldn't desert Leg. Two bright red spots stained Leg's cheeks, and Alice looked at her anxiously. Leg was altogether too excited. She began unfolding the papers. "Nothing but a scrawl on this one . . . What a fool, this one says, 'Better watch out.' Nothing . . . nothing. What in the world—" she broke off suddenly. She peered at the slip she was holding, turned it over incredulously as if it might bear some explanation on the back, then stared at it again.

It was then that the evening nurse, whom Alice did not

know, rushed in. She was just back from her break and heard what had been happening.

She snatched the paper from Leg's hand and read aloud in a hushed voice, "You old witch, you keep out of this, or you'll be sorry."

17

THE NURSE took the note. Next day Mr. Bell paid a personal visit to Mrs. Daniels. Alice was there when he came, but she realized that even she couldn't be dense enough to hang around. But she was back the minute he disappeared into the elevator.

Leg was sitting in her wheelchair. She sucked in her lips when Alice came in, which she could do very effectively since her dental plate had disappeared again.

" 'What'd he say, what'd he say?' " she chattered, imitating Alice's supposed thoughts.

Alice just looked at her. Mocking Alice was going too far, and Leg knew it.

"Well," she said in her usual voice. "He's going to call a meeting, too. He calls it 'coming to grips with the situation.' Says he'll arrange to keep a guard on me night and day, but that I must never presume to interfere with his nursing home again." Leg got away from herself again and put on Mr. Bell's commanding air. "I need have no fear: God (or Mr. B., same thing) will watch over me. But I am on no account to get in touch with my relatives."

Leg pounded her stick a few times. "I hate to follow his

orders, but I certainly won't get in touch with my relatives. They'd make such a fuss, and they might transfer me, just when things are getting interesting. But we've got to get in touch with somebody outside. I don't trust Mr. Bell. This is a very wicked place, this nursing home; and this particular scene is a very smelly scene. We're a great team, you and I, even though I am a damaged old woman, and you an inno- cent—that is the old term, and I like it—young girl. But I think we need reinforcemnents. You'd better get in touch with Mrs. Hones, and it wouldn't be a bad idea to tell Jim."

Alice was solemn, but felt exhilarated. She was still *in on* things; but she wasn't sorry to think of having strong allies.

First she looked for Jim. She felt different about him now. In her excitement and—yes—fear, she lost her doubts and thought of him as she had at first, as strong and resourceful.

"Jim!" she saw him as soon as she had burst out of the elevator on the therapy floor. "Jim, did you hear?"

Ginger Man looked at her in the still, expressionless way he had assumed since the change-of-floors fiasco. He gave a quick, scornful shake of the head. Of course I didn't hear, and why should you ask? he seemed to say. Leg was right. He could express a lot without a word.

"Somebody threatened Leg," said Alice. "It was about this stealing class. Mr. Bell put a guard on her. I have to call Mrs. Hones now."

She rushed back into the elevator. She had work to do. If Ginger Man could tell you things without speaking, he should be able to understand what other people were think- ing, too.

158

She dialed Mrs. Hones's number, but the phone was answered again by the young airy stranger.

"I want Mrs. Hones!" Alice said indignantly.

"I'm afraid you're out of luck, honey," drawled the indifferent voice. "She's not working here any longer."

Alice felt as if the whole phone booth had fallen through the floor. No Mrs. Hones! Why, Mrs. Hones had always been there! Mrs. Hones was *her* social worker.

Alice went numbly back to Leg and told her what had happened.

Leg was put out, but not down. "We'll have to handle it ourselves, then. We'll get Jim's advice. What *they* will do, I don't know—Mr. Bell might just sweep it under the rug, after scaring everybody. Say, though, I wonder if Mrs. Hones was kicked out because she took your side against Mr. Bell. That stinker. It figures he'd make trouble for her if he could —she's always taken too much interest in the patients."

Nurse Boston put her head in the door. "All aides are called to a meeting in Mr. Bell's office."

"But I can't leave Mrs. Daniels," said Alice. "I'm guarding her." She hoped she might get by with this. She didn't want any more of Mr. Bell's meetings.

"I'll stay," said Nurse Boston. "Go along with you, now. And don't worry too much. We've been through these hassles before." She gave Alice a friendly smack on the bottom. Alice didn't altogether like friendly smacks on the bottom, but it did tell her that Nurse Boston was on her side, probably because of Mrs. Hones.

Everybody was gathering in Mr. Bell's office. Nobody looked at anyone else. Alice, however, looked at everybody, feeling free to stare, because she was as usual invisible. Nobody was wondering if Alice had done it, because they knew she was too dumb to steal. Was she too dumb to steal? But it was dumb to steal. It would take a dumb person who thought he was smart. Like that silly Billy Lass.

Was Billy Lass that dumb?

Alice stared at Billy Lass, who was chattering more than anybody else, first with the person on one side of her, then with the person on the other. Acting as if nothing were wrong.

Appolonia, on the contrary, was standing against the wall, her arms folded across her chest. Her eyes were brooding off into the distance. Petrie and Jacques stood next to her, then finally squatted on the floor, as Mr. Bell stalked sternly into the room and stared at them all severely from behind his desk. But Appolonia continued to stand.

"Is everybody here?" asked Mr. Bell. "Mrs. Leaming, call the list."

So Mrs. Leaming, in a nervous tone, called the list. "Appolonia Allen, Jacques Ben Prince, Francine Bray . . ."

Of course they were all there. How could they help being? Except Nurse Boston and someone who was ill, a few part-time aides, and of course, the cooks.

"Stealing," said Mr. Bell, sounding a little like a preacher, but not quite—like an imitation preacher, "is one of the crimes that wrongs our fellow man, and yet can creep up on a person, especially in a setting like a nursing home, where many people seem to have things they don't need or even notice. So, I am always prepared to deal with petty thievery—candy, small items of clothing, toilet articles. But lately, things have gotten a bit more serious. When TV sets

160

are taken at night, when the laundry is looted of a large quantity of towels and bedding, and when somebody sees a truck at the laundry-room door—then it becomes a felony, and we have to do something drastic about it."

The silence seemed to hum, like high wires in a wind.

"I have not called in the authorities, yet," said Mr. Bell. "It would be much better if we could solve this matter by ourselves. So I am calling on the guilty party to make a clean breast of it."

A clean breast, Alice thought—a strange phrase. But then, when you thought about it, they meant making your heart (which was in your breast) clean and honest. It would certainly be nice if somebody would do that. She almost felt like doing it herself.

But nobody did.

"All right, then, if you won't take the good way, the easy way, we'll have to go about it the other way," said Mr. Bell. "We'll have to ask if anyone knows anything about anybody else that might be suspicious."

Another silence.

"Come on!" Mr. Bell's face was turning red.

Alice thought, I'm stupid, but *I* know that if he wanted someone to confess, he should have let them do it privately, like Leg did.

"It's going to be hard on all of us if I have to call the cops!" Mr. Bell said threateningly.

Suddenly there was a rustling sound, and everybody craned to see who it was. Billy Lass was struggling up from the floor. "I know something, but I ain't sure I ought to tell," she said.

Before she could go on, Appolonia's strong voice cut

across her uncertain mumbling. "I know what she going to say. She did see me one night sneaking in after a late date. I didn't want to ring and wake everybody up. I didn't have a key to the laundry-stair door, but I knew I might be late, and put a Band-Aid on the latch before I went out. Of course, I had nothing to do with any stealing."

"How we gonna know that?" said Browny, breathing hard with excitement. "You do that once, you could do it again. Don't look good to me, huh, Mr. Bell?"

"Oh, I wouldn't quite—" Mr. Bell was flustered. "It was right to tell, but I'd need more evidence than that."

" 'More evidence than that'—what a gas!" said Petrie in a deep, angry tone. "Appo! She'd never steal; much too high and mighty."

"Yeah?" said Appolonia, without looking at Petrie. "If you want a get me outa here so bad, Mr. Bell, why don't you just fire me? You can't really pretend to think I'd steal two TV sets and the laundry!"

People almost laughed. Appo, stealing TV sets! Whereas the thought of Appo fixing the door so she could come in late seemed quite logical.

But, if going through the laundry-stair door was so suspicious—Alice looked at Browny and then quickly away again.

Browny had said, "Nobody can keep me out."

Browny looked odd. He was nervously lacing and unlacing his fingers.

Alice's heart began to batter at her chest.

She knew Browny had a key to the laundry-room stair.

But she couldn't possibly stand up and tell. Everybody would look at her.

They would think, "What a dumb crumb!"

But that had been for *not* speaking.

"A person who is dumb is not a crumb," Leg had said. She meant that if you did something nasty (like not introducing Appolonia to her family) you were dumb, but not a crumb. But if you *did* know . . .

Alice stood up.

"Mr. Bell," she mumbed. Nobody heard or even noticed that she'd stood.

"Mr. Bell!" she said again, and then shouted, "MR. BELL!"

"Yes, Alice." He looked annoyed at the interruption. "What, now?"

"Browny has a key to the laundry-stair door," said Alice.

18

ALICE had never dreamed of such a thing as rooming with Appo. Things certainly happened funny.

After the surprise of Alice's telling about Browny, everyone had crowded around her, and everyone had seemed very pleased, except Browny, of course, and Billy Lass Holder, who both said how could you trust what Alice said. But Mr. Bell said that she, Alice, didn't know enough to lie. Which was true.

Appo was especially pleased. She said to Alice, "You're not a dumb crumb!"

Alice liked that. She thought about saying, "You're not a fucking black ass," but she decided it didn't sound right.

Appo put her arm around Alice's shoulder, and they walked down the hall together. "We've got to tell Leg all about it," Appo said. And of course, Leg took all the credit.

"Well, finally," she said. "Why didn't you listen to me in the first place? You two could learn a lot from each other."

"I guess maybe that's true," said Appo, after a moment's pause.

For several days, Alice caught Appo looking at her. But not the way Francine looked at her—as if she were a dog

164

or a cat or a strange piece of furniture. Appo looked at her as if she were a real person. Appo even talked to her.

Still, Alice scarcely knew how it happened that when Francine finished her course a few days later and left, Appolonia moved in. Nobody asked Alice about it beforehand. But by that time, nobody had to, for she and Appo were friends.

Alice shivered a little when she thought this thought, but it was true. She had never had a real friend before—something always spoiled it. And now to have a friend like Appo!

Rooming with Appo was like putting on magnifying glasses and earphones. Everything was larger and clearer and more exciting than ever before. And it was a good time for that to happen.

Browny was gone, and Billy Lass was gone; and there was a queer unsettling feeling around that other people might be gone, too, before long. But not, this time (and that was what made it so queer) aides or orderlies. High-up people. Who and just why, nobody knew, or at least, Alice didn't know, but she suspected Appo knew; and she knew Appo would tell her at the right time, so she would know too.

Nobody else was talking now, either, though people did talk more to Alice. "To think that you were the only one who knew Browny had a key," they said to her. Almost with awe.

Alice usually didn't answer anything to this, but only smiled modestly. But to Appo she said, "That's because he thought I was too dumb to matter. And I was, too, till they accused you."

"You aren't so dumb," said Appo. "In some ways, you see more than other people."

Alice was flabbergasted and couldn't accept that. Now that she was living with Appo and learning so much, Alice was mostly astounded at the things she *hadn't* seen and didn't know about.

The night Appo told Jacques she had a headache and couldn't go out with him, and then sneaked out with Petrie, Alice was very mad. For the first time since they had become friends.

Of course, she said nothing about it, in fact she said nothing at all about anything; and though this had been her invariable condition on all occasions before rooming with Appo, she had lately, in the shelter of their room, sometimes been quite a chattering person (usually about the patients), and always an eagerly listening person, sitting up in bed when Appo came in to hear all about the date, class, dance or movie, or whatever Appo was about. Appo was taking a course in podiatry and studying hard, but she didn't let this cut out her social life, and so she never stayed home a single evening except when she was on duty.

But this time when Appo came in, the light was off, and even when Appo turned it on, Alice remained stubbornly asleep with her back turned.

"Hey!" said Appo, when her noisy undressing left Alice still inert. "What's with you?"

No response.

"Oh, I get it. You're mad about me lying to Jacques. Well, I should have told the truth, but he's such a sweet thing I couldn't bear to."

"He's nicer than Petrie," said Alice, still with her back turned.

"Well, yes, he is nicer in lots of ways," Appo admitted, turning off the light and getting into bed herself. "But he's a foreigner."

Alice said nothing, but she thought things. She didn't know quite how it was related to the dumb crumb incident, but she felt sure it was, somehow; yet she hesitated to bring that up.

Appo brought it up. "If you think I'm prejudiced, like you were about me, you're crazy. It's just that Jacques is from a different ball game altogether, and if he wants to go out with me, and Pan, and you (probably), he wants to do it partly just to try to dope us out. But he doesn't pick up on our signals, or really know how to treat us. He ought to marry a Haitian girl. And he probably will."

"But you said you don't have to marry everyone you go out with," said Alice, for Appo had been working hard to get that point across.

"Right. That's why I'm willing to date Petrie, that mouthy stuck-up goon. Get this: he thinks he's going to be a psychiatrist. Medical school ain't enough for our boy Petrie. Psychiatry, yet! Why, that nut could get into male nursing and really do some good. Ugh!" Appo flounced over on the other side and then gurgled deep in her throat. "But he is a great gorgeous hunk, isn't he? So why shouldn't I go out and have fun with him?"

"I bet you've dated every orderly and—and assistant therapist in this whole nursing home," said Alice.

"Why, you dog! You cunning, underhanded dog!" Appo

cried, after a moment's silence. "You're pumping me about Ginger Man!"

Alice wouldn't answer.

"Well OK, if you can ask for it, you can take it. Yes, I did have a few dates with Ginger Man. And if you think he has nothing on his mind but books and therapy, you can think again. He's a hell of a guy with the girls—there's something special about him. I guess because he can't talk the usual way, and you get curious and kind of sympathetic. But he can sure get a message across by touching. But don't get me wrong, he's not a bad guy. I dig this business of therapy."

Alice stayed awake a long time, turning over in bed carefully so as not to let Appo know. So, maybe he wasn't as handicapped as she had thought—afraid and holding back. But— ". . . a hell of a guy with the girls"! Then that deep look and that smile she'd thought was specially for her was really for just anybody.

The next day the doom that was hovering over the nursing home fell.

Alice was helping Miss Johnson downstairs for a taxi ride to the hospital to visit her niece. Only, it wasn't the hospital now. The niece had been moved into a nursing home only a few blocks away.

Nurse Boston was going along.

"If you want me to act overjoyed, Alice, I'm sorry," Nurse Boston snapped, as she watched Alice swathe Miss Johnson in shawls and pat the thin white waves of hair into place. "I'm glad she's going—I'm truly glad you're going, Miss Johnson—but of all days to get word from Mr. Bell—a royal command, of course—that I must drop everything for two

168

hours and take her! There's Mr. Burket in acute melan-
cholia, I may lose him to state hospital if I can't keep him
quiet; and Mr. Carpenter gasping for breath in this damp
weather; and a dozen other crises."

Miss Johnson and Alice smiled at each other. Fuss, fuss,
fuss!

Nurse Boston went ahead to get the taxi, and Alice
pushed Miss Johnson's wheelchair carefully out of the elevator.

"At last, and it's really your doing, dear," said Miss
Johnson. And just then the door opened, and Mrs. Hones
rushed in.

"Oh, Mrs. Hones!" Alice was delighted to see her and
bursting to tell her all that had happened.

But Mrs. Hones only gave the two of them an absent-
minded nod and hurried straight to Mr. Bell's office, where
she knocked on the closed door: rat-tat-tat! and then burst
through it.

Alice had to go back to her own task, helping to insert
Miss Johnson, arms and legs all sticking out and bumping
into the doors, into the front seat of the taxi, which had
scarcely driven off (Alice still standing and looking after it
with a sense of joyful accomplishment) when another car
drove in under the porte-cochère.

Two strange men and a terribly important looking woman
got out. They, too, went straight to Mr. Bell's door, but it
was opened for them before they had time to knock. Mrs.
Leaming watched like one in a trance.

Strangers often had appointments with Mr. Bell; mostly
the children (or parents, as Alice thought of them) of the
people who needed to come to the nursing home.

169

But what with all that had happened and been rumored, and what with Mrs. Hones bursting in first (after a whole month's absence, caused, at least they said, by Mr. Bell's having complained about her), it added up to excitement.

At lunchtime, heads were together; everybody was whispering. Alice was sure Mr. Bell's visitors were the topic. But this time, nobody told her anything, not even Appo; and Alice decided the last weeks of her being included were just accidental and temporary.

Miss Johnson came back exhausted, and not so happy as Alice had expected her to be.

"The poor dear girl is really in bad condition," Miss Johnson said faintly. And when Alice had gotten her into bed (she was too tired to eat lunch) she said, "She didn't recognize me!" And began to cry.

Alice sat and stroked her hand until she went to sleep—it took only about three minutes. And then went on sadly to tell Leg about it.

Leg wasn't interested. "Oh, that's the way it goes! You turn yourself inside out for these poor old biddies, and they never appreciate it. There's always something wrong with what you've done for them." Alice looked to see if Leg was laughing, for it certainly sounded as if she were talking about herself, but the one subject that was seldom funny to Leg was Leg. "Say, did you hear about Mrs. Hones coming to see Mr. Bell?"

"I saw her," said Alice. "Why do you suppose she wanted to do that?" She was still disappointed about Mrs. Hones's brushing past her in the lobby.

"I think there's something very interesting going on," Leg answered. And when Alice waited hopefully for more, Leg wouldn't go on, but said, "Now, brush my hair a bit, will you?" And she began to repeat poetry, her kind of poetry, never letting Alice get in a word.

When Alice went out again into the hall, she noticed that it was almost empty. When she passed the activities room, Maria called out, "Where is everybody, do you know?" Maria knew even less than Alice about what was going on, because she couldn't keep her mouth shut.

Alice shook her head. The stillness was so puzzling that her curiosity was revved up still further. Maybe they were trying to keep her in the dark, but she wouldn't let them. It was an off-day for therapy, and she'd *just bet* they were down in the therapy room having what they called a BS session.

She got there just in time to hear Appo say: "Up the Fuzz! Long live the Pigs! And all other Stinkers!"

Then Appo saw Alice poised at the door.

"Hey, we forgot to tell Alice! Alice, here's to you! You had your share in the greatest event of the year. Guess what? Mr. Bell's been fired!"

19

ALICE never did quite get the straight of it. But she did gather that her running away and the stealing episode had alerted the county to other ways in which Mr. Bell was mismanaging his job. Mrs. Hones, familiar with the situation and suspicious of Mr. Bell, had been deputed by the county to write up a report, easy to document from her own files, and get the officials to look into it.

A new administrator had come, named Cap Whitby. He was short and thin and lively, very nice to everyone.

"I will say he's systematic," said Nurse Boston, staring at the duplicated sheet of *Requirements for the Week* that had appeared on all desks the very first Monday morning he was there.

"And honest," said Mrs. Leaming, which sounded odd to Alice. Had Mr. Bell, then, not even been honest, and if so why had Mrs. Leaming been such close friends with him?

But two days later, when Alice met Mrs. Leaming in the elevator, she was weeping. When she saw Alice, she pretended she wasn't.

Alice said nothing. This was the kind of situation where

she still felt totally inadequate. But Mrs. Leaming couldn't help bursting out, "He's no gentleman!" Alice still couldn't bring herself to ask what was wrong, though Mrs. Leaming would certainly have told her.

She told everyone else, and Appo passed it along to Alice that evening. "He fired her!" said Appo. She laughed. "I can't help enjoying it. He didn't fire her as a receptionist, but only as a social worker, which she always pretended to be but ain't. Now she's down to typing, which I guess she does well enough."

"Well," said Alice. "Isn't that a good idea, then?"

"A great idea," said Appo. "And I hear he's bringing on a recreational therapist, or occupational therapist, or something like that. It's about time. It's mandated."

"What's that?"

"State law. We've been in violation for months. Only thing is, we're in violation of lots of things. What's he going to change next?"

This question must have been coming up in everyone's mind. Alice could feel it damping down the first chorus of relief over Mr. Bell's departure and praise of the new boss. He scared them.

Alice was scared. She had always wondered if they were right to give her this job; everybody had wondered, from Mike at the home to Mrs. Hones to Nurse Boston and Appolonia. Perhaps *she* was mandated. (She didn't quite understand the word.)

The next shock came when the new therapist arrived and turned Maria out of her beauty parlor. Mrs. Prezinski had blue hair and a dignified manner, and she cleared out Maria's litter of beauty aids, not with her own hands, but efficiently by delegation, within hours. (Now Alice would never have that hair-do.)

Maria went to Cap Whitby, and everybody knew it; and she came out of his room weeping, packed up everything, and left.

"She wasn't fired," Appo explained. "Just downgraded. He said she could help with the crafts, but that she hasn't the right kind of license for beauty work. She couldn't take it. Too bad. Maria will be missed."

On the other hand, the physical therapists were happy. When Alice escorted Miss Johnson to her session a couple of days after these upheavals, Mr. Pitz met them rubbing his hands with joy.

Alice looked around anxiously. Where was Ginger Man? Besides, what was that pile of lumber doing in the hall?

"Look what's happening to us, girls!" Mr. Pitz cried joyfully. "We're being reevaluated, renovated, rejuvenated! We're going to have a whirlpool bath! Appreciated at last!"

Ginger Man came in with a workman, both of them absorbed in a sketch the workman carried. Ginger Man was writing things on his pad. The workman was reading them and nodding. "Yeah. Yeah. That's right. I think that would be an improvement. Say, you know something about building, don't you?"

Ginger Man shrugged, smiled. He included Alice in the smile, with a special little wink added. But—he smiled at everyone.

A real in-training course was set up for aides and orderlies, and the first session gave even Alice some new ideas. "Just what I always advocated," said Leg.

But when Alice came to her room the next time for the hair-brushing ritual, Leg was wild. She sat in her wheelchair in front of her chest with all the drawers wide open, throwing all their contents on the floor.

"I'm going home," said Leg. "I shall not, will not, must not submit to these indignities any longer. Alice! Call Son. Tell him to come and fetch me no later than six this evening."

"What's happened?" asked Alice, automatically bending to pick up the assorted underwear and other objects—banana peelings, notebooks, perfume bottles, peanuts and papers that always got mixed up together in Leg's drawers.

"It's my teeth," said Leg. "He told me—that man—that so-called administrator—that impostor—that scavenger—that I was not allowed to have teeth. I said, keeping my calm, I suppose no new glasses, either, although these are obsolete to the point of analogy with prehistoric monsters. He said, 'Right, no more glasses.' He said, 'It's a part of my policy to cut out foolish extravagances.' So that's what it is —to be able to see, to speak clearly, to chew one's food— foolish extravagance!"

Alice laid a neat pile of folded clothes on the dresser, and Leg immediately snatched them and sent them flying.

"The man's whole philosophy is an open book to me now! I'm amazed that I was deceived for an instant! He's a man of things, of systems, of analysis; he cares nothing for people; they are less important to him than the figures on their social security cards. He is inhuman. A Hitler. A Caligula . . . why don't you go and make that phone call to Son?"

"I will as soon as I can," said Alice.

175

Must she? She approached Nurse Boston, bent over records. "Nurse," she said timidly.

"Hush! Hush! Later!" Nurse Boston raised her hand but not her eyes. "I've got to get this report done—unless you're telling me someone's dying."

Appo was gone for the afternoon, taking a patient to the eye clinic. Who else was there? Alice's heart went up, down, then up again. It was Thursday. Ginger Man was there.

The confusion in therapy was terrific, the noise, the sawdust, and the congestion, but the patients were bright-eyed and interested. Mr. Pitz was suffering. "Careful! Careful! Please, Mrs. Levy, watch out for that board."

Ginger Man was helping a patient in the parallel bars. Alice went right up to him and stood there until he noticed her. With her face directly in front of him, she said: "Jim. Leg is all upset. She says she can't have teeth or glasses. Could you come up? She says she's going home."

Jim watched her lips, and then looked into her eyes. They weren't thinking of things like smiles and touches, though, they were thinking of Leg. Jim held up his hand, fingers extended, twice. (Ten minutes.)

Alice nodded and went upstairs. Leg was worse.

"Did you phone? Did you phone?" she was screaming. Nurse Boston had had to leave her records and was standing, frantic and disgusted, at the door.

"What a spectacle you make of yourself," she said to Leg. "You, such an intelligent woman."

"Mean you're in favor of this Nazi regime?" Leg yelled. "Take the gold out of your teeth and melt it down! Throw the broken glasses on the road to perforate the tires of the liberators!"

176

She saw Alice. "Did you get him? Is Son coming?"

Alice reluctantly shook her head. "But I went and got— I got *him*," she said. She was lost between "Ginger Man" and "Jim," could only find the pronoun, which seemed to her clear enough, when given sufficient emphasis. *"He's* coming."

She saw Leg look over her shoulder. She saw Leg's contorted face flush scarlet.

"Oh, you traitor," Leg cried in a kind of gasping whisper, her eyes glaring sidewise at Alice. "You *fool*."

And Mr. Whitby, not Jim, came into the room.

20

Jɪᴍ came right after. No more than the ten minutes he had promised. But Leg was out of it by then, exhausted to the point of coma; sedated and helpless. So quiet she looked dead. Mr. Whitby had not had a chance to say a word before she collapsed.

Jim stood silently by Nurse Boston's desk while the story was told and retold, but didn't make a sign. After half an hour, the subject had been worn to rags; everything to be said had been said. People drifted away. But Alice and Jim still stood there, unsatisfied, distressed.

Jim reached over the counter and felt around till he found a pad and pencil. He wrote on it and put in front of Alice.

MEET ME IN THE LOBBY AFTER DINNER

There was no question mark. Alice looked at it a minute with her mouth ajar, then automatically closed her mouth and looked up at Jim. She made no answer. But Jim smiled, gave a little wave, and went away.

She had made no answer because her mind was still not clear of Leg's attack. "You traitor! You fool!" She put Jim's note in her pocket to deal with later.

Little by little, his message developed itself on her mind. What should she do? Ask Appo? Appo was on watch over Alice, after hearing what had happened with Leg.

"Where you going?" asked Appo, in the elevator after dinner, as Alice pressed the button for first floor.

No, she didn't want to ask Appo. Alice jerked away and got out in the lobby.

Ginger Man was already there, and suddenly her mind cleared. She must tell him. She must show him she knew about all those other girls.

"I can't go with you," she said. "You don't want *me*."

He nodded firmly. "You have to," he said. "Besides I do." Even though the words did not travel the usual way, from his throat to his mouth to her ears, he said them; and she heard them, and she believed them.

They went outdoors and walked a little way down the drive, under the trees they had seen in bud and early leaf, now heavy with summer. They stopped and stood still for a moment, and then Ginger Man took hold of Alice's arms, facing her. He held them gently, and they stood there several minutes face to face, a few inches apart. Though he didn't say anything, she knew he was trying to tell her not to worry about Leg.

Alice's head tipped up so she could look into his face. Though it was dark, she could see the shape of his forehead, cheekbones and chin. His eyes, invisible, were looking into hers, invisible.

Finally he drew her nearer and kissed her lips.

His mouth was firm and warm. His lips didn't tease hers, as movie stars' did in TV, or gnaw or writhe. They pressed steadily, strongly, and ever closer, and his arms and her

179

arms bound the two of them into one. Time stopped moving forward and instead went down inside her, into depths she had never known were there, and up also, like the wine she had tasted at Appo's birthday party.

Then he let her go, twined his fingers in hers, and walked her back to the door. Then he gave her hand a strong grip and let it go. He opened the door for her, and they went in.

They looked at each other smilingly. Alice looked at the broad forehead, deep-set eyes with their corner sprays of smile-wrinkles, wide mouth, firm chin, reddish curly hair and ears that stuck out a little. She liked it all. He was looking at her in the same delighted way. The elevator came, and Alice looked once more and went up.

She felt very peaceful. Maybe he had kissed lots of other girls, and maybe he'd kiss lots more. Maybe he'd kiss her again, and maybe he wouldn't. But what she knew was that he had kissed her and meant it.

Leg was better next day. She sent for Alice early in the morning.

"Don't go down there," Appo said, as she carefully combed her Afro. "After somebody's insulted you, you can send a substitute. You're entitled."

"I'll go," said Alice.

Appo looked at her with a line between her brows. She'd been trying to comfort and reassure Alice ever since last evening and gotten nowhere. Alice knew she seemed completely blank; Appo was afraid she was wiped out.

"She didn't mean anything," Alice said, to comfort Appo.

"C'mon in, hurry," said Leg briskly when Alice appeared. "It time to bru' my 'air."

Oh dear, oh dear, the speech was much worse. Leg must have had another stroke.

"Yeh—hit me 'gain," said Leg. "Funny, i'nt—ain't it. Now Whitby got gi' me pla'! An' now ca' taw an'way!"

She reached the brush out to Alice.

"Thi' ti' you be' do the po'—po'—"

"Poetry," said Alice. "Yes, I will."

She took the brush—now so worn that it hardly penetrated even the thin ravellings that were Leg's hair—and began to stroke it gently over the old pink skull.

"On the shores of Gitchee Gumee . . ."

(She's tired of that; I better learn some of those she really likes, Alice thought.)

Son and Joyce came. "My dear child," said Joyce. "I heard. I heard. How can we apologize and thank you enough?"

"Oh, come, Alice is sensible," Son put in, as usual saying it so well it sounded as if he were quoting himself, rather than just saying something. "She understands the aged and their shortcomings."

Mr. Whitby came.

Leg eyed him calmly, her bundle-of-stick hands folded on her chest. "No need worry ovah tee' an' gla'—'pectacle—now," she said.

"Oh, you'll be better soon," said Mr. Whitby. "We'll take up the teeth and glasses with the doctor." He glanced at Alice. "In fairness, I must assure you that you did this young lady an injustice yesterday. Unfortunately, she did *not* come for me, or inform me in any way of what you were saying."

"Ne' mind," said Leg. "Good 'colding never do nobody no harm." She held up her right forefinger instructively. "Know wha'? Bad grammar be'er in t' o' t'ouble."

"I'm not sure scolding is what is required," said Mr. Whitby. "Scolding might improve the intent, but not always the performance."

He wasn't looking at Alice, but Alice was sure he was talking at her; she didn't know quite what he meant, but it lay on her mind. Did he want to get rid of her. Was that it?

"What's the matter, kid? Leg's better, and she's not mad at you at all," said Appo, later.

Appo kept saying things like that to Alice for several days. Then she was called in by Mr. Whitby for a conference.

"What did he want?" Alice asked when Appo came back.

Appo didn't look at her. "Oh, nothing."

Alice could guess. Mr. Whitby hadn't forgotten that she hadn't come to him, but had gone to Ginger Man, when Leg was so mad. And yet, she was too sad to do anything. If she was to be fired, she would be fired. Maybe it was better. She wouldn't have to wonder any more about Jim. He smiled now whenever he saw her, and some day, she thought, he would give her another note. But she didn't know what would happen after that.

One night she looked at the want ads in the paper. She'd have to get another job. Mrs. Hones or somebody would help her, but she'd like to have some say, this time.

The summons came next morning. It came to Nurse Boston and was passed from mouth to mouth. "Mr. Whitby wants to see Alice in his office at eight o'clock."

Pan was the one who ran after Alice with the message. "Gee, kiddo, I hope— Come back and tell us right away, won't you?"

Appo watched her go in. She said, "I'll wait."

But nobody could go in with her.

Mr. Whitby sat behind the desk, somehow more scary, in his neatness, his rightness, and his certainty, than that false-face Mr. Bell had ever been. He stood up politely till she had sat down.

"I think you realize, Alice, that employing you here was always something of an experiment," said Mr. Whitby.

"Nobody ever told me that," said Alice.

Mr. Whitby looked a little surprised. "No? Well, I suppose not in so many words."

"If I'm so stupid—and I suppose that's why you're firing me," said Alice, "then they *should* have told me in so many words. They shouldn't have let me go on so long thinking it was all right."

"Yes, I've been realizing that for some time," said Mr. Whitby. "The fact is, helpless old people need especially expert care. And the general idea of who can give this expert care is—well, a stereotype. Well-trained, experienced, mature people are what's needed. You came here as a very young inexperienced person; and you're still very young, and in many ways, unqualified."

"Retarded," muttered Alice past the lump in her throat. "You mean you can't trust me." The tears were prickling the back of her eyes and would soon fall out, no matter how hard she tried to keep them back.

183

"No, no, no," said Mr. Whitby quickly. "No, I was only saying that appearances . . . inspecting officials prowling about . . . relatives looking the place over . . . wouldn't realize . . . In reality, you are almost more than adequate. Your one serious problem in dealing with the old folks is that you go along with their delusions, you pamper them. Particularly Mrs. Daniels."

"I like Mrs. Daniels," said Alice, rubbing the tears viciously off her cheeks with the back of her hand.

"Of course; she's a wonderful old lady. But she does suffer from a chronic brain syndrome, and when she gets into one of her contrary phases, it's unwise to indulge her—maybe even unsafe."

"The others make Leg yell—is that good for her?"

"We-ell," said Mr. Whitby, "in the long run, it probably is."

"What long run?" asked Alice. She thought of Mrs. Tree, who had already died, and of Miss Johnson, who would be dying soon. All of them—even Leg. She gave one hard sob. "They have to be happy *now*."

There was a sudden knock at the door. Instead of saying "Come in," from his chair, as usual, Mr. Whitby sprang up and went to the door.

It was Mrs. Hones.

"Have you fired her?" she cried. She was out of breath, and she looked mad.

"We've been talking things over," said Mr. Whitby.

"Well, I think you ought to reconsider."

Mr. Whitby rubbed his nose. He didn't look at Mrs. Hones. "I guess maybe I am reconsidering," he said. "I never really had a chance to talk with Alice before."

" 'To really talk with Alice'?" Mrs. Hones repeated. "Very few people ever do." She looked curiously from one to the other of them. "With Alice, actions speak louder than words. And that suits the old folks fine. Doesn't that mean something?"

Mr. Whitby, cool as a cucumber again, gave a little shrug. "Nurse Boston bears you out. She has apparently reversed her own first judgment about Alice's inadequacy. But what about emergencies? You know that lots of things come up that Alice isn't equipped to handle. And you have to face it, that's the kind of fact that looks very bad in black and white."

"On reports, you mean. Actually, things come up that *nobody* can handle. Anyway, this girl—there's something special you should realize. I've learned a lot from the records about her family. Her mother had, probably, about the same mentality as Alice."

Mrs. Hones turned away from Mr. Whitby. She stopped trying to convince him and began talking wholly to Alice . . . Oh, what would she say? Would she answer that terrible question, the one Alice hadn't dared to ask?

"You and your mother are really much alike. She cared about everyone—but especially about you. When she found out she was going to die, she decided it would be better to give you up. And, honey, you're getting to be just like her —good and respected, and with a rare gift for love."

What was "a rare gift for love"? Alice didn't quite get it. "Good and respected," she sort of understood. And "especially about you"—she knew what that meant.

Alice gave a big gasp to get some air in her lungs. She hadn't breathed for quite a while.

Then she looked over to see what Mr. Whitby would say.

Whatever he said didn't matter too much. She'd found out what she really needed to know. And she was strong enough, sure enough, to face anything she had to. Good and respected, like her mother.